The Mail Order Bride of Cheyenne

Vanessa Sarlson

Published by Trellis Publishing, 2021.

THE MAIL ORDER BRIDE OF CHEYENNE

First edition. July 11, 2021.

Copyright © 2021 Vanessa Sarlson.

ISBN: 979-8224572267

Written by Vanessa Sarlson.

THE MAIL ORDER BRIDE OF CHEYENNE

VANESSA SARLSON

Chapter 1

Plumes of black smoke rolled into the sky as workers emerged from the factory, exhausted. Daisy was one of them. Her fingers were worn from work and her arms ached with a deep, never-ending fire.

"Brutal in there, isn't it?" Her co-worker, Maggie walked beside her. "And the union takes most of our hard-earned money and for what? When my pops died, they didn't give us a dime." She snorted.

"You shouldn't bad mouth the company so loudly," Daisy warned. "If a foreman should hear you..."

"Oh, poppycock, what do I care?" She grinned like a madwoman. "Today was my last day."

"They sacked you?" Daisy stopped, eyes wide.

"Oh, no, dear, I sacked myself.

Daisy furrowed her brows together with confusion. "I'm not sure I understand." As they walked toward the center of town, a couple of men whistled in their direction. They looked at the girls with hunger in their eyes. It made Daisy shiver. Most of the men in town were good-for-nothing lowlifes and she wanted nothing to do with them. But, if she continued to make pennies on the dollar, she had no chance of supporting herself. She'd be forced to marry just to survive.

Maggie grabbed a nearby rock and threw it as hard as she could. It glanced off a nearby horse and spooked it. The giant animal reared on its hind legs, front legs kicking the air.

"Think you're tough, girlie?" The leader of the group crossed the street first. "I like me a girl with a bit of fight." He grinned, leaning forward like he planned to kiss her.

Suddenly, Maggie swung her purse as hard as she could.

Thwack!

The man stumbled, seeing stars.

Daisy couldn't stop herself from giggling.

"Oh, you think this is funny, do you?" He growled. "I'd be careful if I were you..." The color drained from her face at the sound of his threat. All jokes aside, they'd be no match for the group of hooligans.

"Lay a finger on her and I'll be the death of you lot." Maggie snarled.

The group hackled in amusement. "The mouth on this one!" The leader slapped his knee as he laughed. "But maybe she's a little too feisty. I think maybe we should teach her a lesson."

Maggie clutched her bag but her confidence was starting to wane. Luckily, a patrol officer blew his whistle just in time. The sound was enough to send the gang packing. "Ladies, are you alright?" He asked. "Did they do anything to hurt you?"

"No, not at all." Maggie brushed a strand of hair behind her ear like it was no big deal. "Thank you, officer." With that, she hooked her arm around Daisy's and off they went to their boarding house. "What a bunch of peckers." She scoffed. "That's why I'm getting myself a *real* man." She boasted with a smile that stretched from ear to ear.

"What are you talking about?" Daisy feared that her friend had lost her mind. "Have you met a suitor?"

"I *found* a suitor." She corrected. Once they were inside her room, she opened her drawer and pulled out what appeared to be a newspaper. "It's a special issue of the *Times*."

"Who are all these men?" Daisy asked. "And... women too."

"You see, *Wedding Chimes* is a mail-order-bride service." Maggie snatched the newspaper and opened up to the third page where one man, in particular, was circled with black ink. "That there is my future husband."

"What in tarnation are you going on about?" Daisy pressed her hand against Maggie's forehead.

Maggie slapped it away. "I'm moving out west."

Daisy shook her head. "You can't be serious."

"Oh, but I am." I fell back into her bed and sighed a contented sigh. "I'm finally going to leave this poverty-stricken life of ours. After tonight, I'll never have to deal with this rat-infested building or our nasty foremen. I'll have a house of my own and a husband to provide for me." She spoke with a certain dreaminess to her voice.

"But, do you even know this bloke?"

"Not exactly. I've seen his picture and the description he wrote about himself. That's good enough for me." She turned and leaned on her elbow. "Don't look at me like that, darling. This is everything I've ever wanted. Besides, everyone knows that western men are perfect gentlemen. They're nothing like the crooks around here."

Daisy shook her head and sat down on the edge of the bed. "Are you really leaving?"

"Tomorrow. On the morning train." Maggie squeezed her shoulder. "But, don't you worry. I've found you the perfect husband too." She giggled as she turned the newspaper to the final page. "His name is Rex."

Curious, Daisy glanced over her friend's shoulder. Sure enough, Rex was particularly attractive. He wore a wide-brimmed cowboy hat. Even so, tuffs of dark hair slipped around the edges. It looked nice and thick. His eyes matched the hair. They were deep and soulful. His jaw was strong and well-defined.

"See, you like him already." Maggie jumped to her feet and grabbed some writing materials. "Here, I want you to write him a letter. Don't even bother to wait on his response. It might be months before it gets back to you and by then, another missus will have beat you to it."

"But, I have no idea who this man is. What if I find out I'm not fond of him?"

"Oh, trust me, anything is better than this rat hole." Maggie forced the pen into her hand.

"Let me sleep on it."

"By then, it might already be too late," Maggie warned. "But, I suppose I can't force you to do anything." She grabbed a towel. "I'm going to try and take a bath." And, with that, she vanished from the room, leaving Daisy to contemplate her future.

A roach scuttled across the wall, nearly scaring her half to death.

Maggie was right.

Anything was better than this god-forsaken place.

Chapter 2

"Excuse me, sir, but do you know how long it'll take us to reach Wyoming Station? Specifically, Ruby Gorge." Daisy hailed down a conductor. After countless hours of travel, she was starting to get a little restless.

"Shouldn't be long now. Perhaps another hour or so." He informed. "Are you visiting family?" He had noticed her luggage bags. "Women rarely travel this far west on their own." There was something of suspicion in his voice.

"Y-Yes, family." She stuttered, faltering under his gaze.

"You take care of yourself, miss." He tipped his hat in her direction before continuing down the train and into another cabin.

Daisy looked out the window at the passing wheat fields. The mid-morning sun was slowly approaching its zenith, casting a warm glow over the land. She smiled. At least nature made her feel optimistic. So, she kept her head held high and rode through the remaining hour.

***

But when she arrived at the train station, there was no one there to retrieve her. She waited and she waited and she waited. Dusk settled on the land and she became the last person standing on the platform.

With no other choice, she picked up her luggage and started into town. There, she found the postmaster locking up shop for the day.

"Excuse me, sir!" Daisy rushed forward.

The postmaster turned and raised an eyebrow. To her surprise, it was a woman. She had a stocky frame and broad shoulders. And, instead of a dress, she wore a pair of loose-fitting wranglers.

"Ma'am." She corrected with a sigh. "What can I help you with, miss?"

"I'm new in town and I'm looking for someone."

"And who might that be?" She asked. "I know everyone in town so I reckon I can give you a hand."

"Rex Hardin."

"Hardin?" She repeated. "You're looking for ol' Hardin? Don't tell me that he finally found himself a wife."

Daisy nodded. "That's why I'm here."

The woman laughed. "Oh, now isn't that a hoot. And I had my bets on that man being a bachelor all his life." She shook her head. "Well, come on, I'll give you a lift to his ranch. I'm sure he'll be more than happy to see a doll like you at his doorstep. God knows he's tired of seeing my weathered old face."

Daisy followed her to a single-horse carriage. Awkwardly, she climbed to the top. As soon as the wheels started turning, she felt extremely uncomfortable. The wooden structure groaned with every bump and jostle. Daisy feared it would collapse at any second and yet, somehow, they made it to the outskirts of town. There, the postmaster followed a dirt road for a mile. At the end of that mile was a sturdy-looking log cabin. Behind it was a wide expanse of land. Some of it was used for farming while other parts held corrals for horses. Daisy could just about make out their frolicking forms.

"Well, here we are. I would stay and introduce you but I have a family to feed back home." She cracked her reins and before Daisy could respond, she was already gone.

The young girl's heart thumped like a wild stallion. Her palms prickled. Beads of sweat gathered at the back of her neck.

Suddenly, the door swung open. Rex stopped dead in his tracks. He did not expect to find a beautiful woman standing at his doorstep. "Can I help you, miss?" He asked.

"Oh, um, are you Rex Hardin?"

"I am." He answered while adjusting the brim of his hat. Doing so, their eyes locked for the first time. Daisy's heart skipped a beat and for a moment, she forgot how to breathe properly. "Is there a reason why you're here? I've never seen you around town before."

"I just arrived, today," Daisy explained. "I... I answered your ad, the paper – *Wedding Chimes*." When she was met with a look of confusion, she reached into her bag and pulled out the newspaper clipping. "I sent you a letter but my friend told me that I shouldn't wait for your response."

Rex took off his hat and ran his fingers through his thick hair. "That would have been the smart thing to do because I posted that ad in error." He admitted. "I'm not looking for a wife."

Daisy's eyes grew so wide that she feared they would bug right out of her skull. "You're not?" Her voice was barely a whisper. She had used up all of her savings to make the trip. If this man did not need a wife then she was up a creek without a paddle. "Are you sure?"

"Yes, I'm sure." Yet, despite his words, he stepped forward and picked up her luggage. "That being said, I'm not going to leave you out here. The least I can do is provide some lodging for the night and then we can get you back on the train in the morning."

Daisy shook her head. "I can't do that."

He ushered her inside with a hand pressed against the small of her back. His touch sent a rush of energy through her veins. In an instant, all her worries melted away. She looked up at the cowboy and for the first time, she felt safe in the presence of a man. "Let me get you some tea and then you can explain your situation, alright?" He offered her a warm smile that seemed to pierce into her very soul.

She sat down beside the fire and while he busied himself in the kitchen, she admired his home. It wasn't much but it was certainly cozy. Even so, she could imagine how lonely it must be to live all on one's own.

Rex returned and handed over a hot mug of tea. "Now, care to explain why you can't go back on the morning train?"

"I used all my money to get here..." She admitted, cheeks reddening with embarrassment. "Perhaps I should have given this whole thing a bit more thought."

"Maybe so." He agreed with a nod. "But there is nothing you can do about it now." He bent down and added another piece of wood to the fire. With the poker, he moved it around a bit until he was satisfied.

Daisy watched his every move. Something about this man was highly mesmerizing.

"Look, I'm not looking for a wife but I could certainly use some help around the ranch."

Chapter 3

The following morning.

Daisy had a difficult time falling asleep that night. She kept tossing and turning on the unfamiliar bed. The moonlight crept through her window, illuminating her room with an impossible brightness.

By the time the sun started to peek over the horizon, she was already in the kitchen making breakfast.

Rex appeared in the doorway and cocked his head at the young woman. "What are you doing?" He asked.

She jumped, startled, and nearly dropped the skillet she was holding. "Oh! You're already up!"

"Of course I'm up. There's plenty of work to be done around here. I can't afford to lazy around." He grabbed a few slices of bread from the counter. To his surprise, they were already toasted with a good slathering of butter. He smiled at the rich taste. "But, I suppose I could make some time for breakfast."

"Good. I was hoping you'd say as much. I really appreciate you letting me stay here even after the misunderstanding. I wanted to do something to show my appreciation." As she spoke, she placed a plate of eggs in front of her new employer.

He grabbed his fork and shoveled quite a bit into his mouth.

Daisy held her breath. She had never cooked for someone else before. Personally, she liked her own food but that didn't mean that others also would.

"Mmm, these are some mighty fine eggs if I do say so myself." He continued to eat with an hungered fervor until his plate was wiped clean. When he was done, he rubbed his stomach with a satisfied smile. "I think with that, I'm ready to work if you are."

***

Daisy found herself stepping into a barn for the first time. The smell was pungent. She had to hold her breath just to keep herself from getting sick.

"You'll get used to it." He said as he opened up a stall door. Inside was a small mare with a pair of gentle eyes. "We're going to start with Jasmine. She's a calm soul. Wouldn't hurt a fly so she'll be perfect to train you with."

Daisy nodded. "Just show me what to do." She inched forward, eager to learn.

"Now, I want you to keep in mind that this is dangerous work. Horses are creatures with a will and mind of their own. If they don't like what you're doing to them, they'll let you know."

She bit her bottom lip. "How dangerous?"

"A good horse kick can send you to an early grave. And some of my bucks here are still wild. I rounded them up from the countryside. I would stay away from those until your proficient. I wouldn't want you getting hurt."

Daisy nodded.

"But, I don't mean to scare you." He handed her a brush. "To start, I want you to brush Jasmine's hair. Approach her slowly. That's it. Now, how out your hand so she can sniff you. The faster she learns your scent, the faster she'll learn to trust you."

Jasmine sniffed her hand with a huff of her nostrils.

"Alright, now try and pet the side of her neck. She licks a bit of scratching right behind her ear."

"Like this?" Daisy asked. As if to answer, Jasmine whinnied and shook her head with contentment.

"Just like that. I think you two will get along just fine."

***

For the rest of the day, Daisy was tasked with taking care of Jasmine. By the end of it, she was exhausted but it was a good sort of exhausted. Her work felt meaningful, unlike the work she performed at the sweatshop.

"How are you making out?" Rex leaned against the stall with a grin on his face. He couldn't keep his gaze on her face. The way she was bent over accentuated her lovely backside. He drank in the sight of her before finally looking away, face slightly red.

"I'm just about done, I reckon."

"Well, here are your wages for the day." He handed over a crisp two-dollar bill. "When you start performing some of the more complex tasks, I'll be sure to pay you accordingly."

Daisy shook her head. "I can't even begin to accept this."

"Why not? You earned your keep fair and square."

"It's too much." She was used to making a couple of cents each day. $2 was nearly her weekly paycheck back home.

"Take it." He folded the bill into her hand. "I ain't never seen a girl work as hard as you did today." He stepped inside Jasmine's stall and took Daisy's hand. "Come, I want you to meet the star of my flock, so to speak."

At the end of the barn was a horse as dark as night. His coat was so sleek, it looked like satin. He shook his head sending it white mane flowing down his neck like a shock of snow. "Calm down, Shadow, it's just me." The animal stamped at the ground.

"I don't think he likes me very much." Daisy was hesitant about approaching the animal.

"He's still a wild one." Rex rested his hand on her shoulder. "I'm working on taming him but he's proving difficult."

The horse stepped forward and shot his head over the rim of the door. He snorted and nuzzled against the woman in an affectionate manner. Daisy laughed and rubbed his neck just like she had with Jasmine. "It seems I make have spoken too soon."

Rex watched curiously as the stallion flicked back his ears, tail swishing with pleasure. He had never seen Shadow acting this way.

Daisy reached into her pocket and pulled out a sugar cube.

This was a mistake.

Seeing the treat, Shadow lurched forward, snapping at her hand. His sharp teeth broke her skin with ease, sending crimson droplets into the hay beneath her feet.

She recoiled back but the sight of her injury was enough to make her woozy. The world spun at a dangerous pace. She tried to blink it away but instead of helping, it only made things worse.

Rex caught her before she could hit the ground. "Whoa there. I got you. I got you. Easy now."

Chapter 4

"Luckily, it isn't very deep. You should be fine in a day or two." Rex spoke softly as he wrapped her hand with a bandage. "I would take you to the doctor but he's in the next town over."

"Thank you." She whispered.

"Why are you thanking me?"

"Because you've been nothing but nice to me since I've gotten here. You could have sent me back but instead, you offered me a job..." She avoided looking him in the eye. "And now, you're taking the time to take care of me."

"Of course." He lifted her hand to his lips and kissed her knuckles. "I'll always be here to take care of you."

***

A few months later.

Daisy was quickly getting a feel for the ranch. Rex was confident about letting her handle most tasks from gathering hay to feeding the horses. Still, whenever she was close enough, he would always keep an eye on her.

He wasn't looking for a wife but he was certainly growing fond of the charming young women. His father had warned him that women were nothing but trouble. And he could never remember his mother so he had always assumed the worst of her. But, Daisy? She was different. They had yet to argue. He loved her demeanor. And she had the cutest smile in all the west.

"I'm gonna get us some lemonade," Rex announced, popping his head into the barn to find Daisy polishing some of the saddles. "And maybe when we're done for the day, I can finally get around to teach you how to ride."

Her eyes widened. "Do you mean that?"

He nodded. "If you're a ranch hand, you should learn how to ride."

"I would love to." She waited for him to leave before putting down the bottle of polish. If she was going to learn how to ride, then she wanted to ride Shadow.

She opened his stall and he immediately trotted up to her. After the initial incident, Daisy was cautious but Shadow was turning out to be a gentle giant. "Hey there, buddy." She cooed as she gently rubbed the side of his neck. "What do you say about going on a ride with me this afternoon?"

He nuzzled her pocket.

"Hungry, are you?" She pulled out a carrot and he took it right out of her hand. "That's it. Now, I want to clean out your hooves so you're nice and comfortable when we go riding. Is that okay?"

She grabbed a nearby stool and the cleaning instruments. Shadow seemed complacent enough so she grabbed his back leg and rested his hoof on her lap. As soon as he brought the pick to his sensitive foot, he reacted.

Kick!

Daisy went flying through the air and landed in a large pile of hay. A deep, unspeakable pain shot through her chest. It felt like her ribs had shattered, piercing into her heart. She wanted to breathe but her lungs no longer seemed to work. A warmth soaked through her dress and when she looked down, it was painted with a crimson rose.

Crumbled under her body, her legs lay twisted. Her ankle was already swollen. There was no way for her to get up.

Nearby, Shadow nibbled on some oats as if nothing had happened.

"Rex...!" She yelled in a feeble whisper but the shout didn't make it very far. "Rex!" She tried again to a similar effect.

Suddenly, he appeared with a pitcher of lemonade in his hand. "Daisy?" He called out when he didn't see her.

"In here..."

He rushed over to Shadow's stall. "Oh my, what happened?"

"I tried to clean his hoof and he landed a kick right in my chest."

"Does anything feel broken?" He asked with an expression washed over with concern.

"Everything."

"Hold on, I'm getting you to the doctor." Rex maneuvered his arms underneath her body but the second he moved her, she cried out in pain. "Shh, shh, it's alright, baby. Everything is going to be just fine. I just need you to hold on, okay?"

Her mind no longer functioned, wiped out by the agony. She blinked and a series of events developed before her eyes. *Rex carrying her back to the house. Rex hitching her onto the horse. A bumpy horse ride that seemed to stretch into an eternity. The setting sun. An old woman's voice. Rex shouting.*

What was he saying?

"I don't care if the doctor is about to win a thousand dollars in a poker competition." He growled. "Because, by God, I will drag him out here by the waistband of his birches if it comes down to it."

"Please, sir –"

"No, I don't want to hear your excuses. I *love* this woman, you here. I love you. And I'll be damned if she doesn't survive long enough for me to tell her that."

Daisy tried to stay awake. Did Rex love her?

No. That couldn't be. She was just his employee. He wasn't looking for a wife. Her mind swirled with these questions until she felt herself becoming incredibly woozy.

The rest of her strength left her body and she crumbled off the back of the horse. She would have hit the ground and broken her neck if it wasn't for Rex's strong arms catching her just in time.

"Oh God..." He whispered. "You're not going to make it..."

Chapter 5

A few days later.

Daisy woke up to a room that was warm and misty. A strange scent wafted through the air. It was strong enough to make her cough. Doing so sent a burning pain through her chest. It felt like someone was staging a dagger right between her ribs and into her heart.

She cried out but the sound died halfway up her throat.

Tears blinded her vision.

Suddenly, she felt a strong hand squeezing her own. "Shh, it's okay. I'm here now." Gently, whoever it was, brushed back her hair. A second later, they pressed their lips against her forehead.

Rex.

Her heart seemed a beat, forgetting about the pain. "R-Rex..." She tried to say but her lips were incredibly dry. It was like having a mouthful of sand.

"Here, drink up." He pressed a mug against her lips. "This will help."

It was sweet at first but then came an incredibly powerful kick that burned her entire throat.

"Jesus, what is that?"

He laughed. "A shot of moonshine with some honey. The doctor said it would get you talking and by golly, he was right." Rex reached out and cupped her cheek in his hand. "You had me praying for a minute there. We weren't sure if you were going to make it."

Their eyes locked. Daisy blushed. Then man genuinely cared about her and she cared about him.

"Rex, I need to ask you something."

"And, what might that be?" He cocked an eyebrow in question.

"Right before I blacked out... I thought I heard you say something..." Before Daisy could finish speaking, a tall man dressed in a white vest walked into the room.

From what she could tell, he was covered in blood and it frightened her.

"My apologies. Poor bloke had a run-in with a couple of bandits. They nearly blew his arm off just to snag a couple of bucks." He shook his head. "Some people are nothing but savages."

Daisy turned pale. "So, is that *his* blood?"

The doctor looked down as if he hadn't realized he was covered in blood. "I suppose so. We were forced to amputate."

"Amputate?" She repeated, horrified.

Rex held her hand and shook his head. "Please, doctor."

"Right, my apologies." He walked up to the bedside and placed his hand against her forehead. Luckily, he had washed his hands. "Looks like the fever is gone. She's awake." He leaned forward and stared into her eyes. "Pupils look normal."

Daisy could feel his rancid breath on her lips and she hated it.

"If you'd like to take her home, you're more than welcome to. I'd suggest a few months of rest. And I'll prescribe a pain remedy that you can pick up at your local apothecary."

"Thank you." Rex got up and paid the fee. It was quite the stack of cash and seeing it leave his pocket made Daisy feel incredibly guilty about the whole thing. She should have been more careful.

"Let me just give her a shot of the medicine now so she'll be numb for the right."

***

Daisy wasn't just numb, she was knocked out. By the time she woke up, she was settled against the fireplace and swaddled in a heap of blankets.

"Good, you're awake. I just finished making us some soup. I'm sorry. It's probably not nearly as good as what you usually make but it's something." He held out the bowl but Daisy was so fatigued she couldn't even lift her arms to take it. "Right. Let me." He said as he started to spoon feed her, neglecting his own supper to do so.

She wanted to protest but he wouldn't allow her to. He just smiled that heart-warming smile of his and continued to take care of her.

When her bowl was emptied he finally turned to his own.

Daisy watched him. "Rex." She finally said. "Do you love me?"

The question came so abruptly that the rancher nearly choked on his broth.

"I do not know if I had heard it in delusion or if you actually meant it." Her cheeks were so red that they matched the hue of the fire.

He placed his bowl on a nearby table and answered her with a kiss. It took Daisy by surprise. Her body stiffened at first but soon she melted against his warmth. He ran his fingers through her soft, silky hair as their lips continued to dance like old time partners.

Both their hearts thumped like a couple of drums.

Daisy's lungs burned for air but she did not dare pull away. It felt much too good to stop.

But finally, they were forced to breathe. Rex lingered with his forehead pressed against hers. "I was raised to believe that all women are vile. My own mother ran away from my father shortly after my birth to be with another man. He always told me that she had turned his life into a living hell and I didn't want the same to happen to me." He paused and pinned a strand of her hair behind her ear. "But after I met you, I soon learned that my father was wrong. You aren't vile. You're the most beautiful thing this life has to offer."

"Rex..."

Tempted by her innocent, pink lips, he kissed her once more. When he pulled away, he held her face in both hands and looked into her eyes. "I love you, Daisy, and I'd be the happiest man in the world if I could call you my wife."

Daisy honestly didn't know what to say.

"Now, I would ask you to marry me but I won't do that."

Her heart stopped.

"It's dangerous out here. The horses are a threat. Bandits raid the land. Drunkards carry guns. This is no place for a lady and after almost losing you, I can't ask you to stay."

Daisy felt the tears starting to roll down her cheeks. "Are you telling me to leave?"

"I could never do that but I'm giving you the option. Go back to the city where it's safer." He took her hands and squeezed them. "Because I can't bear to lose someone I love."

"Neither can I," Daisy whispered as she wrapped her arms around his neck. "So, please, don't make me leave. I want to stay here with you. I don't care about the risks. They'll all be worth it if I can call myself your wife."

"Is that truly what you want?" He asked, holding his breath as he waited for an answer.

"More than anything."

A bright grin painted his face. "Then, let's get married!"

Epilogue

Two years later.

"I think tonight's the night," Daisy said with a knowing smile on her face.

"Oh?" Rex returned the smile. "What makes you say that?"

"I can feel it in the air." She nodded. "And nine months from now, we'll be bringing our very first child into the world." As she spoke, she rested her head on her husband's shoulder.

In front of them ran a bubbling brook. The horses enjoyed the crisp, refreshing water, tails swishing.

"I bet I can beat you to that there bush over there." Daisy pointed to a small gathering of trees in the far distance.

"I think you've forgotten that I grew up with horses all my life. I'm a much better rider." He boasted. "And I will not let my wife prove otherwise."

"I think you're scared because you know Shadow's a much faster horse than Diesel."

"Diesel is a very reliable horse." Rex protested. "He has never let me down before."

"Then, what are you so scared of?" Daisy continued to tease her husband.

"Maybe I'm scared of you getting hurt." He took her hand and kissed the back of it. "You worry me sometimes with your recklessness."

"Nothing is going to happen to me, I promise." She leaned forward and kissed his lips. "Now, quit being such a worry wart."

"I have a better idea." He got up and hitched Diesel to a nearby tree. Then he jumped onto Shadow's back.

Daisy furrowed her eyebrows together, clearly confused. "What are you doing on top of my horse?"

"I want to show you something. Hopefully, we'll be able to see her tonight."

"Her?" Daisy repeated. A pang of jealousy pierced through her heart. "Who are you talking about?"

"You'll see." He held out his hand for her.

She hesitated for a moment but she nonetheless grabbed it.

Rex hoisted her onto the horse with utmost ease. A second later, they charged through the open fields.

Daisy kept her arms wrapped around his torso. His body radiated a deep warmth that made her feel safe and sound. She nuzzled into that warmth and smiled to herself.

It didn't take long for them to approach the mountains. They loomed overhead like giants.

Rex continued to press Shadow forward.

"Where on Earth are we going?" She asked.

"You'll see." Again, he answered with the same mysterious phrase.

And then, suddenly, he stopped. Daisy squinted against the darkness, trying to notice something of significance.

"Do you see her?" He whispered.

A flash of white caught her attention. She whipped her head in that general direction and gasped. It was a beautiful white horse with a mane as pure as snow. There wasn't a single blemish on her entire body.

Shadow snorted at the sight of her.

"We're going to catch her," Rex said.

"How?"

"Do you still know how to maneuver a lasso? I taught you a couple weeks back." Rex jumped down and tied Shadow against a nearby tree. "Stay here, buddy, we're gonna get you a fine-looking lady friend."

Shadow stomped the ground in answer.

Meanwhile, Daisy had already grabbed the coil of rope from the saddle bag. She tied the lasso just as Rex had taught her to. Then, she started to spin it over her head in a nice circular motion.

"Good, good. Now, I'm going to stand over here and I want you to try and reel me in."

Daisy giggled but she nonetheless complied with his request. Once she had her aim, she launched the lasso in his direction and it went right over his head. She tightened the rope and pulled him with all her might.

Rex stumbled forward and their lips collided. Unable to keep their balance, they both fell to the ground.

Daisy laughed. "I am the luckiest woman in the west."

"Well, I'm the luckiest man in the world." He kissed the tip of her nose with a smile. "You've done nothing but make my life rich and colorful. I couldn't ask for a better partner in crime."

They were just about to kiss when Shadow reared his head and undid the knot holding him in place. Like a bolt of lightning, he shot toward the white female horse. She waited for him at the top of the mountain, head held high.

Daisy watched as Shadow nuzzled against his neck. "Now we really need to bring her home with us or Shadow will never forgive us."

Rex groaned. "Catching one horse is hard enough but two..."

"Don't worry, I know we can do it." Daisy kissed his cheek for encouragement. "Besides, I learned from the best."

He chuckled and before she could walk away, he grabbed her by the wait and reeled her into his body. Gently, he kissed the side of her neck.

She blushed crimson. A shiver of joy ran through her spine.

Then, his lips traveled onto her earlobe. He nibbled it. "I love you." He whispered ever so softly.

Those three words were enough to make her heart jump out of her chest. "I love you, too, Rex." She lassoed her arms around his neck and smiled. "And, I'll never stop loving you." Their foreheads came together. "Until death do us part."

AMISH SECOND CHANCES

STEPHANIE SWIFT

Sarah stared longingly out the front window of the farmer's market and sighed. Only four days remained until Christmas and the sidewalk was packed with shoppers rushing to find last-minute gifts. Multi-colored lights glowed from the store windows across the street, and the snow was just starting to fall.

Any other time, the picturesque view would've made her excited for the holiday, but right now it was just giving her a massive headache. Unlike last year, she would be spending this Christmas alone, and that was enough to make her want to cancel the holiday altogether.

Sarah shuffled her feet against the tile floor as she made her way to the door so she could lock up. It had been a long day, and she was worn out – physically and emotionally. After listening to the happy chit-chat between her customers all day, she craved the peace and quiet of her apartment, where she could curl up on the sofa with a book and a steaming mug of coffee and not have to worry about the outside world... at least for a few hours.

Before she reached the door, however, it was suddenly flung open by two elderly women, Mary Martin and Ruth Coleman, whom she recognized from the Amish community on the outskirts of town where she'd once lived – before the divorce...before her life was turned completely upside down.

"Forgive me, Sarah!" Mary called. "I know you're getting ready to close, but I just need to buy a couple of things, and I promise I won't take long."

She wanted to push them back out onto the sidewalk, but they were rushing through the store before Sarah had the chance to object. She knew the Christian thing to do would be to bite her tongue and turn the other cheek, but it was difficult when these same two women were among the ones responsible for spreading rumors while she and her ex-husband, David, were going through their divorce proceedings.

Sarah went to the check-out counter to wait on them. She busied herself sorting through receipts and tidying up around the cash register, but she didn't miss the sideways glances the two women cast her way as they walked up and down the grocer aisles. They spoke to each other in soft whispers, and even though she couldn't make out the words, Sarah knew without a doubt she was the topic of conversation, which made her blood boil.

Nothing ever changed.

After what felt like an eternity, Mary and Ruth made their way to the register, and as Sarah rung up their items, she kept a smile glued to her face but avoided eye contact as much as possible.

It's almost over, Sarah. Just get them out the door and you can go home and relax. Be nice.

"We've missed seeing you in church the past few months," Ruth remarked. "How have you been?"

Sarah stood up a little straighter and squared her shoulders.

Here we go.

"I've been doing well. Just staying busy with work. How about you?"

They looked at each other again, and as Sarah put Mary's cash in the register and bagged her groceries, she caught the two of them exchanging smug smiles, which raised another red flag.

"Oh, we have no complaints," Ruth replied. "Sarah, I hope you don't mind me saying that we were all stunned when we learned David was still seeing that...that *woman*. I mean, the very nerve of him doing such a thing! I know you must be devastated."

It felt as if the wind had been thrust from Sarah's lungs as she leaned against the counter to keep from falling into a broken heap on the floor. David was still seeing Ann, the woman he was unfaithful with? No, that couldn't be true. He wouldn't do that.

Or would he? She thought he'd never cheat on her, but she'd been sorely mistaken about that too.

"Well, don't you worry, dear. We're on your side – always," Mary intervened, before giving what Sarah assumed was supposed to be a comforting pat on her hand. "*Denki* for letting us sneak in past closing time. I hope we see you at church this weekend for the special Christmas service."

She wanted to respond, but for some reason her mouth couldn't form words, so she nodded and smiled instead, which seemed to appease them. Mary picked up her groceries and the two of them headed for the entrance. When Sarah caught them snickering on their way out, she rushed to lock the door behind them before she received any more unwelcome visitors.

With the store finally empty, she flipped the business sign in the window to "closed" and turned off the lights. She could faintly hear Silent Night playing on the overhead speakers in the clothing store next door, and it was all a bit too much. Since the divorce, she'd basically existed on the hope that David was alone and regretting what he'd done to ruin their lives. Knowing he was happily existing with the woman he threw her away for was a kick in the gut...and heart.

Sarah leaned against the wall beside the window so she wouldn't be seen by the people walking past. The snow was falling faster now, and it wouldn't be long before everything was covered in a beautiful white blanket. Thoughts of her and David snuggling together on the front porch swing of their old home, watching the first snow of the season, flitted across her mind and made her eyes tear up. It was one of the traditions they'd looked forward to each year, but the first snowfall of this season had long come and gone, and she'd spent it alone, locked away inside her apartment.

Sarah pushed the thought from her mind and tried to imagine something happier. In a few short days she could take down the Christmas decorations. The holiday would be over with, and she could put it behind her and move on to a new year full of hope and possibilities.

It was small, but at least it was something to look forward too.

* * * *

David brought the truck to a stop in front of Palmer's Market and turned off the engine. The brick building loomed in front of him as he took a couple of deep breaths to calm his nerves. It was his first day making deliveries, but that wasn't what had him so anxious. It was also his first day back in the city.

When he took the part-time delivery job, he never expected to end up in the city limits of Lancaster – much less in the middle of Main Street. He was content to stay in the small town of Amory, twenty miles east of Lancaster, where he worked in construction full-time and kept to himself on his days off.

But being away from work gave him too much time to think about things that were better left alone, and so he took the part-time job.

Now he rarely had time to sit and think and that was a good thing – a very good thing.

David picked up a crate of milk jugs from the truck bed and walked to the front door entrance of the market, propping the crate on his hip momentarily so he could open the door. A bell chimed when he stepped inside, and he was immediately bombarded with several different aromas that assaulted his senses all at once, including bell peppers, celery, tomatoes, cinnamon and vanilla. The fragrances made his stomach growl from hunger, and he silently chided himself for leaving that morning without having breakfast first.

He spotted an employee helping a customer on the opposite side of the store, but her back was turned, so she didn't notice him walk in. David carried the crate of milk to the checkout counter and set it down. While he waited, he thumbed through a couple of magazines on a rack near the register, but it wasn't long before he heard footsteps approaching. He also heard what resembled a gasp, and when David looked up he was surprised to find his ex-wife, Sarah, staring back at him.

Over her clothing she wore a green apron with Palmer's Market stitched in bright yellow lettering across the front, and David groaned as he sent a quiet prayer to the heavens, asking the Lord to please open the floor and swallow him whole. If he'd known Sarah worked at one of his delivery stops, he never would've taken the job in the first place.

"David? What are you doing here?"

He didn't answer right away, and they stared at each other for the longest time, stopping only when the customer she'd been waiting on cleared her throat in a nonchalant way of letting her know she was ready to be checked out.

Sarah broke their gaze and went to the cash register, and David instinctively closed his eyes and inhaled the lavender scent of her shampoo as she walked by. At least, in a world where everything felt so uncertain, there was one thing he could rely on and that was Sarah and her obsession with lavender-scented beauty products.

She was just as beautiful as always, but she looked very different than the last time he'd seen her. The Amish attire he was used to seeing her in was replaced with a denim skirt and a purple floral-print blouse, and her hair wasn't hidden beneath a white bonnet anymore. Instead, it cascaded in soft auburn waves around her shoulders, and he could have sworn he saw a touch of make-up on her eyes and cheeks.

When the customer paid and left, there was an awkward silence between them, interrupted only by the tick-tock of the cuckoo clock on the wall behind the counter. He didn't know what to say or if he should try and start a conversation at all. Perhaps it would be best to just get the money for the milk and be on his way.

"You're making deliveries for Paul now?" she asked.

David followed her gaze to the crate and nodded. "He expanded his business, and he doesn't have time to make the deliveries himself, so I'm helping out a couple of days a week."

The conversation felt stilted and forced, but he didn't know how to change that. He was honestly surprised she chose to talk to him at all, especially since they hadn't parted on the best of terms.

"I'm sorry, Sarah. I know you said you never wanted to see me again after the divorce, but I honestly didn't know you worked here. If I did, I never would've taken the job."

He noticed the way she clenched her jaw, as if she didn't like his answer, but it was the truth. The last thing he wanted to do was make her angry or uncomfortable.

Sarah opened the register and removed some bills before slamming the drawer shut. When she thrust the money in his face, he took a cautious step backward to keep from being hit.

"Here," she said. "I'll let Mr. and Mrs. Palmer know they need to find another milk supplier. I'd hate for you to see me against your will."

David furrowed a brow as he took the money. "What is wrong with you? You're the one who said you never wanted to see me again. I was just trying to apologize."

Sarah leaned over the counter and he could see the fury blazing in her beautiful blue eyes. Even though the store was empty of customers, she kept her voice low, but there was no mistaking the way her voice trembled and seethed.

"You act like this is such a burden for you, but how do you think it makes me feel knowing you're still seeing Ann? Do you have any idea how humiliating that is for me?"

David's jaw slacked as he held up a hand to keep her from saying anything else. "Whoa...wait a second. What are you talking about? I'm not seeing Ann. I haven't seen or spoken to her since you and I went our separate ways."

She was speechless at first, but he detected something else in her gaze that made his heart thump a little faster. Relief, perhaps? He knew it couldn't be love, because he'd ruined that a long time ago.

"Mary Martin and Ruth Coleman told me you were still with her."

David's face flushed as the anger began to steep in his veins. He should have known those two busybodies were behind something like this.

"And you believed them?" he asked. "Sarah, you should know better than anyone else how much they love to gossip. They're two bitter old maids who have nothing better to do with their time than to try and make everyone around them miserable."

She nodded, but she didn't say anything, and the awkwardness returned. David put the money inside the zippered bank bag Paul gave him and made a move to leave. He'd heard enough, and he wasn't interested in wasting time arguing over nonsense.

"I have four more deliveries to make, so I should be going. I hope you have a Merry Christmas, Sarah."

David turned to leave, but Sarah reached out and grabbed his arm to stop him. The warmth from her touch seared through the fabric of his shirt and sent a shiver racing up his spine.

"I'm sorry, David. You're right. I should've given more thought to where the information was coming from and not jump to conclusions."

The soft lull of her voice pierced his heart, and for the millionth time, he wished he could take back the hurt he caused her – the hurt he inflicted on her and so many other people with his lapse in judgement.

"Are you happy, Sarah? I know you might find this hard to believe, but I truly want you to be happy. You deserve it more than anyone else I know."

He saw tears swell in the corners of her eyes, and he swallowed hard to keep from getting emotional.

"I am happy," she replied.

She looked away when she said it, and he could tell by the tone of her voice that she wasn't being completely honest, but he wasn't about to pry because he knew it was none of his business. For all he knew, she had moved on and was seeing someone else.

David inhaled deeply. The thought of her with another man made his insides twist into a painful knot, so he changed the subject to keep from dwelling on it. "If you'll show me where the freezer is, I'll put this milk away for you before I leave."

Sarah motioned for him to follow her and as he picked up the crate and tagged along behind her, he tried not to watch her every move. Still, it was hard not to notice the way her hair swished around her shoulders when she walked or the way the lights danced off her porcelain complexion. There were many things he missed about their relationship and being able to run his fingertips over her soft skin was high on the list.

"Are you spending Christmas with your family?" she asked.

David opened the freezer and organized the milk on the metal rack by shuffling the older bottles to the front and placing the newer bottles behind them.

"They're spending Christmas with my sister and her family in Ohio. I was invited, but you know how much I hate flying."

She smiled at his comment, and he breathed a small sigh of relief, hoping they were finally past the unease from their earlier conversation. "What about you? Is your family staying at the house this Christmas?"

And just like that, her smile was gone.

"I don't live there anymore," she replied. "I've been renting the apartment upstairs from the Palmer's for about eight months now, and it's too small for guests."

David was stunned. He'd never imagined Sarah not living in the home they built when they were newlyweds. It had always been such a huge part of her life, and she'd spent so much time decorating and taking care of it.

"I don't understand. Did you sell the house?"

Sarah closed the freezer door and began making her way back to the checkout counter, leaving David no other choice but to follow.

"I still have the house, but I couldn't live there anymore. It was too painful," she admitted. "Plus, I was tired of living around such nosey neighbors and being the talk of the town, so I moved here to get away from it all."

He felt another kick to his gut, and he didn't know how to respond. For as long as he lived he would never get over the guilt of kissing Ann and losing Sarah's trust. Add to that the guilt he now felt over Sarah leaving their community to get away from the heartache and it was almost too much to bear. He had been shunned and she couldn't live there in peace. Oh, what he wouldn't give if he could start over and make things right.

"I'm so sorry, Sarah. I didn't know."

A customer walked in before she had the chance to reply, and David took that as his cue to leave. He was so downtrodden and his spirits were so low he could have easily crawled out on his hands and knees.

"I hope you have a Merry Christmas, David. I mean that."

He gave her a half-hearted smile and returned the sentiment before turning to go, and as he closed the door behind him, he peered one last time through the window and watched as she waited on her customer. Would there ever come a day when the guilt wouldn't feel as if it were crushing him?

Somehow, he doubted it.

* * * *

Sarah watched from her second-floor bedroom window as a marching band from one of the local high schools passed by on the street below. It was Christmas Eve and the annual Lancaster Christmas parade was well under way. They were already thirty minutes into the parade and she could still see a lengthy line of floats and bands extending along the length of Main Street and beyond.

Sarah grinned as she watched the children lining the sidewalk across the street jump up and down excitedly when the float carrying Old Saint Nick passed by. He threw candy into the crowd and the kids scattered, trying to grab as much as they could fit into their pockets before someone else snatched it up. It made her laugh seeing how determined they were.

Although the temperature had dropped considerably over the past couple of days, the frigid air didn't appear to dampen anyone's spirits. She was grateful the Palmer's had given her three days off work to enjoy the holiday, but she wished there was more to do besides watching the parade from her lone spot by the window. She could've joined the others on the sidewalk, but it seemed pointless watching the parade by herself while everyone around her enjoyed it with their loved ones.

Sarah blew her warm breath against the cold window and traced a heart in the fog on the glass as her thoughts turned to David. He'd looked so handsome when he visited the store. She was used to seeing him in Amish clothing, but she had to admit that the jeans, company work shirt, and boots made him look more rugged and masculine. His black hair was cut short and he even had a bit of stubble on his face. Since their divorce, she'd often pondered whether he'd settled into a different Amish village somewhere else, but seeing the way he was dressed answered that question.

She couldn't help but wonder if he'd found someone to spend the holiday with since he wasn't able to visit his family. He seemed surprised when she mentioned living in the apartment, and she frowned when she considered the possibility that she might have to sell the house someday. She had no plans to return, and since David had been shunned, there really was no point in keeping it. Letting go of it, however, was something else entirely.

They'd put their heart and soul into building the small wood frame house – right down to the extra bedroom they hoped to convert to a nursery someday. But then Ann entered their lives and everything changed in an instant. She could still recall the night David confessed of their interlude as if it were yesterday, and the pain was still just as raw.

Sarah rested her head against the window pane and thought for a moment. Could she really call it an interlude? They'd shared one kiss that David swore on many occasions was initiated by Ann. She feverishly shook her head. No, a sin was still a sin in God's eyes, whether it was just one kiss or one night of passion, and that one kiss had broken their sacred marriage bond.

A knock on her door startled her from her reverie, and as Sarah went to answer it, she forced the troubling thoughts from her mind. It was Christmas, after all – a joyous holiday meant to celebrate the Savior's birth, and it shouldn't be spent dwelling on parts of her past she couldn't change.

When Sarah opened the door, she found Mrs. Palmer standing on the other side. The elderly woman was dressed in seasonal clothing, from the jingle bells tied to her shoelaces straight to the toy reindeer antlers on her head. The front of her work apron was decorated with a multitude of Christmas buttons and pins, and she caught a glimpse of Grandma Elf stitched across the front of her red and green sweater. She had to admit she looked adorable.

Sarah's grandparents passed away when she was a child, but if she had the chance to choose another one to call her own, Mrs. Palmer would be at the top of the list.

"Good morning, Sarah! Merry Christmas Eve!"

It was rare to see the elderly woman without a smile on her face, and as she wrapped Sarah in a warm hug, she smiled when she detected the faint scent of sugar cookies. It was also rare not to smell some type of savory goodness on her clothes or in her salt-and-pepper hair, since Mrs. Palmer loved to bake and did it often.

"These are for you. Fresh from the oven."

She handed Sarah a small metal tin, and her mouth watered when she lifted the lid and found an assortment of cookies inside. Chocolate chip, oatmeal, peanut butter – and just as she suspected...sugar cookies.

"Thank you so much, Mrs. Palmer. They smell divine."

The smile on her cherub face was enough to melt Sarah's heart, and she felt like kicking herself because she had nothing to give her in return. Having grown up in an Amish household her whole life, she rarely received gifts or material things for the holidays, so this new way of celebrating was something she was still trying to get used to.

"Oh! This is for you too, dear. Someone named David called the store a little while ago looking for you, and I told him you weren't working. I wasn't sure if you wanted him to know your cell phone number or not, so I asked for his number instead."

Sarah almost dropped the cookie tin as she took the piece of paper from Mrs. Palmer's hand with shaky fingers.

"I better get downstairs. We'll be closing early and heading to my granddaughter's house to spend Christmas with her and her family. I'll see you Monday morning."

Sarah hugged her one more time. "Thank you again, Mrs. Palmer. I hope you and your family have a wonderful Christmas."

Mrs. Palmer gave her an affectionate squeeze. "You too, dear."

When they said their goodbyes and Sarah closed the door, she leaned against it for several long minutes, staring at the paper in her hand with David's phone number scribbled on it. The ten digits beckoned like a light in the dark, but she couldn't help but feel a little hesitant.

What could he possibly want?

More than a little intrigued, Sarah went back to her bedroom and retrieved her cell phone from the nightstand beside her bed and punched in the numbers. Her heart beat so rapidly she thought it might pound right out of her chest, and she took a couple of deep breaths to try and remain calm. After two rings, she heard a familiar deep voice on the other end of the line.

"Hello?"

Sarah sat down on the edge of her bed before her wobbly knees landed her on the floor.

"Hey David. It's Sarah. I was just returning your phone call. Is everything alright?"

There was a long pause before he answered, and Sarah worried she may have started the conversation off on the wrong foot. She wasn't used to talking on the phone, and she couldn't even remember the last time she'd received a call from a man other than her father or Mr. Palmer.

"Would you be angry with me if I told you I want us to spend Christmas together?" he asked.

Although spending the holiday with her ex-husband should've been the last thing on her mind, she had to confess she felt a little excited over the idea. Thanksgiving had come and gone with nothing to show for it besides leftover turkey from her dinner with the Palmer's and she'd been dreading Christmas ever since.

"If you don't want to, I totally understand," he continued.

Sarah went to her bedroom window and watched the paradegoers having a good time on the sidewalk below. If she said no, what else did she have to look forward to besides watching the rest of the parade? It would be ending soon and then what was there to do – spend the rest of the holiday weekend doing crossword puzzles or watching television?

"Sarah? Are you still there?"

She turned away from the window and focused her attention on David. "What did you have in mind?"

There was another short pause as Sarah waited anxiously for his answer.

"I would like to cook for you," he replied. "Would it bother you if I buy the ingredients and come over to your apartment to fix dinner for you? If that makes you uncomfortable, we could always have dinner at my house."

Her mind drifted back to the many meals they'd cooked together while they were married and she smiled. She did her best, but she couldn't deny the fact that he was by far a better chef than she could ever hope to be.

"I wouldn't mind if you cooked here."

For some reason, just saying it made her feel giddy inside.

"Great! Can I come over around 5:00 and get started or is that too early?" he asked.

She didn't have to see his face to know he was grinning because she could detect it in his voice.

"Five o'clock is fine. There's an enclosed stairway beside the market that leads to the second floor. When you get here, press the buzzer by the door, and I'll let you in."

They talked a little while longer before hanging up and Sarah remained where she was, mulling over their conversation in her mind. She hoped she hadn't made a huge mistake, but there was only one way to find out.

* * * *

David juggled the grocery bags around in his arms so he could press the buzzer, and he finally managed after a couple of unsuccessful attempts. When Sarah appeared, and opened the door for him, he tried not to laugh as the two of them haphazardly climbed the stairway like two circus clowns trying to stay upright on a unicycle.

"Good heavens!" she exclaimed. "Did you buy the whole store?"

David laughed. "I know...I know. I kind of went overboard."

When they made their way inside her apartment, he followed her to the kitchen and set the bags on top of the counter.

"I get the feeling you're trying to impress me," she said with a wink.

David chucked as he started unloading the bags. "Maybe I am."

As she took the grocery items and placed them in the cabinets and refrigerator, he tried not to ogle her, but she looked so beautiful. The red dress she wore showed off her curves and her hair was tied loosely at the base of her neck with a festive ribbon. She had on lip gloss, and it took every ounce of strength he had not to pull her close and kiss her. He didn't want to assume she'd gotten dressed up just for him, but he did feel a little bit hopeful.

"I know this probably isn't what you'd call a traditional Christmas meal, but I remember how much you love spaghetti," he commented.

Sarah smiled as she retrieved some pots and pans for cooking. "It's always a good time for spaghetti – holiday or no holiday."

When David started preparing the meal, he was pleasantly surprised when Sarah joined in to help instead of leaving him to do it all alone. It felt like old times being in the kitchen with her, and although he worried at first there may be some awkwardness between them, he was happy when that proved not to be the case. They cooked the meal in silence, but it was a comfortable silence, interrupted only by the soft strains of Christmas music streaming from a radio in Sarah's living room.

David took the pot of spaghetti noodles and drained the water in the kitchen sink while Sarah retrieved the garlic toast from the oven, and as they brought their dinner to the table, he thought back to the many nights they'd dined at the kitchen table in their home. He wanted to mention it, but he also didn't want to risk ruining the moment, so he kept his thoughts to himself.

Baby steps, David...baby steps.

David pulled a chair out for Sarah, and when she sat down, he didn't miss the way her cheeks flushed, which he hoped was a sign she was enjoying his company. He took a chance and sat down in the chair beside her, instead of across the table from her, and he was relieved when she didn't object. They both bowed their heads and closed their eyes, and as David said grace over the meal, his heart fluttered wildly when Sarah reached out and held his hand, like she used to do when they were married. Perhaps it was just something she was accustomed to doing, but he took it as a positive step in the right direction.

They talked about the usual things over dinner, like the weather and work, and although David wanted desperately to talk about something more personal, he was determined to wait for the right moment.

"Do you mind me asking if you still attend church regularly?" she inquired. "I noticed you don't wear Amish clothing anymore, so I was curious."

David sat up a little straighter in his seat while contemplating his answer. Could this be the right moment he was waiting for? It felt as if God was opening a door, and he took a deep breath, not wanting to mess up what might be his only opportunity to tell Sarah how he felt. He cleared his throat before attempting to speak.

"My boss invited me to visit his church a few months ago, and I attend services every Sunday. When I was shunned from the village, I was afraid I might lose my way, but my faith in God is even stronger now. I finally realized I don't have to be a member of a certain church to know He loves me and that I'm forgiven."

David held his breath as he waited for her to reply. He hoped he didn't come across as harsh, but it was the truth. When Bishop Tucker and the elders in the village decided to shun him instead of accepting his apology for his indiscretion, he thought his life might never be the same, but he prayed for and received God's forgiveness, and that was all that mattered.

Sarah put down her fork and napkin and leaned back in her chair. She laced her fingers together on top of her lap, and she was quiet for a long time, but when she looked at him, he was relieved to see her smiling.

"I'm glad to hear you say that. After our divorce, I saw a side to the community I didn't like, and that's why I decided to move. I still went to their services every week, but it was never the same, and I eventually stopped going. A couple of women who work at the clothing store next door invited me to their church, and I've been going there ever since."

Her whole face lit up while she talked about it, and it was easy to see what a positive influence it had on her life. It felt as if a weight had been lifted from his shoulders after worrying for so long that his wrongdoing may have affected her spiritual life too, but it was plainly evident her faith was still as strong as ever.

David took a chance and reached out to hold her hand.

"Sarah, do you think there will ever come a day when you will be able to forgive me?"

He half expected her to say "no", but when she smiled at him, he felt a small glimmer of hope.

"I forgave you a long time ago, David. Forgetting what happened hasn't been as easy to accomplish, but I'm working on that."

He sighed.

"So, I'm guessing a reconciliation might be too much to wish for?" he asked.

Sarah placed her free hand on top of his arm and gently caressed his skin, making his heart leap into his throat. Her touch was soft and sent a warm current rushing through his whole body. He was so worried the moment might pass he didn't dare move a muscle.

"I wouldn't say it's completely out of the question," she replied with a grin.

They remained that way for the longest while, simply enjoying each other's company, and when they resumed eating, the conversation flowed freely. His heart soared every time she laughed, and when they began reminiscing about special moments from their past, the ray of hope he clung to seemed to burn a little brighter.

After dinner, as Sarah cleared the table and David cleaned the kitchen, they accidentally bumped into each other, and when he wrapped his arms around her waist to keep her from falling, he was ecstatic when she didn't try to push him away. He probably shouldn't have held on as long as he did, but it felt so good having her in his arms again, and he wanted the moment to last for as long as possible.

"I don't think there will ever come a day when holding you like this doesn't feel perfect and right," he whispered.

She looked up at him, and his heart pounded when he saw the desire in her soulful blue eyes.

"David...do you think it would be possible for us to start over?" she asked. "I don't want to rush this though. If we do try again, I would like to take it slowly."

David traced her jawline with his fingertips, loving the way her body still trembled at his touch. "I believe we can do whatever we set our minds to. I know I hurt you, Sarah, and I'm so sorry, but I promise I will never hurt you again. I hope you know that."

When she stood on her tip-toes and tenderly kissed his lips, David knew he received his answer...and the second chance he longed for.

AN INJURED AMISH HEART

ALICE EVANS

<u>Prologue</u>

Love is more than a feeling. And it isn't something so simplistic as an idea... It is this positive, electric energy that flows throughout your entire body and radiates outward. No matter who you are or what you have experienced, everyone is capable of experiencing this phenomenon. One of the greatest aspects of being human is our capacity to love; but there isn't just one kind of love, there are several facets of love. As I theorize, love isn't something so simple as one idea or definition. Whether it is familial love for those closest to you, or a love so strong it feels like your heart is going to rip right out of your chest for the one person God has designed for you; love is the most powerful source we can ever hope to know.

Unfortunately, there is a flaw in this innocent desire to love. If you ask someone to tell you why they were with someone, the typical response is because their heart told them to and they couldn't think of anything or anyone else. Cheesiness aside, this brings up an issue. Can we trust our heart to make the right choice?

"How do you know when you meet this person that they are the one for you? How can you differentiate the one, perfect person from the sea of hundreds or even thousands? There is no guarantee that the person you meet is the perfect person for you. You may not end up with someone perfect, but you may end up with someone who is perfect for you.

But then again....

What happens when you end up with the wrong person? Whether by proximity or a series of misleading circumstances, and then one or both parties are injured. Keeping your heart in check is one of the hardest struggles a human can face. Because we can't help who we love, and there is no guarantee who our heart picks is someone whose heart will also pick us. Such a thing happened to Lovina Smith. Rain fell upon her window pane, as she continued to suppress her tears. Her mind raced as her final conversation with him flashed before her eyes:

"I'm so glad you were able to come over to see me Luke. It feels like I haven't heard from you in ages. Don't you think that as your betrothed I should get to see you more often?"

"We need to talk, Lovina."

"Oh, I know. We have to start planning; well we really just need to decide where we will be living after we are married. My parents left me this house, which is good sized; but if we want to have kids someday-"

"Lovina!" Lovina was shocked by this sudden change of tone. In the four years they had known each other he had never raised his voice to her.

"L-Luke... what's wrong?"

"I... we... I don't think we fit together like we used to."

"Luke, what are you saying? Do you... do you not want to marry me anymore?"

"Look. I get this probably is the farthest thing from what you expected, but I need to do what is right for me, and frankly this," Luke gestured between himself and Lovina, "isn't doing it for me anymore."

"What do you mean you don't want to get married anymore? Is it something I did? What's going on with you?"

"Exactly what I said. Why are you being so thick about this?" Luke strode towards the door, about to fling it open.

"Well can you at least explain to me why you are doing this? You owe me that much Luke!"

"You know exactly why." Lovina's heart fell out of her chest and onto the floor. As Luke strode back towards her, she could almost feel his footsteps stomp all over the love she had gifted him for so long.

"That's it? What did you find someone else willing to satisfy you?"

"Yes."

Lovina slapped her hands against her window, forcing the memories to stop. The tears, now spilling out of her eyes, caused her to wonder whether it was still raining, or if her vision was just blurring. All the pain she felt, all of love she gave him for four years, all washed away.

"God, please give me the strength.... The strength to overcome."

<u>Chapter One</u>

After that day it became almost impossible for Lovina to notice the passage of time. Days, months, weeks, or even years; she wouldn't have been able to tell. Though days continued to pass, in her mind, she was still stood, frozen, in that room. That plain, simple room that once made her beam with joy. The slatted blonde wood beams and the oaky smell in the air, now forever taint the memories she held so dear. Lovina would stare around the room to see the memory of her father whittling as her mother prepared for supper and she'd once feel a surge of relief. Now...

Now, she can't think about the good times in her home without remembering Luke. From the moment he stepped into her life, that room became the setting. Even in the first moment they met, Luke stepped over the threshold and into her heart. At the time, Luke was her father's apprentice and had taken over her father's business when he passed away three years ago to a bout of pneumonia.

Lovina only ever had one job in her life: working at her godmother's bakery. "Fisher's Bakery" had been in the family for generations. It wasn't a stately building; some may even refer to it as a shack, to which Lovina would quickly defend. To her, it wasn't just a slightly run-down building... to her it was where all the brightest memories of her childhood were made.

Lovina's earliest memories surround her godmother from when she was a little girl; running in after her mother to find her godmother - Cynthia Fisher - covered in white powder and with fallen strands of auburn hair plastered against her forehead. She has no children of her own, so Cynthia's plan had always been to pass the business on to Lovina. Loving her more than her own family, Cynthia watched on as her beloved godchild worked mindlessly behind the counter. Trying to figure out what to do, Cynthia invited two of Lovina's closest friends to discuss options.

"There must be something we haven't tried yet... I mean, she's just... It's like she's not even there anymore."

"I know... she's only been to the store and home for six months. This isn't healthy," Sara Dixon responded. Sara's eyes plead with her friend's frame as she looked on in pity.

"But what can we do? She doesn't want to talk about anything, and she refuses to admit that she needs help," a silken voice replied. Teresa Miller - an old school friend of Lovina's - had come at Cynthia's bequest. She recently had been married and moved to a town a few counties over. However, as soon as she got word that it was Lovina who was in trouble, she had no issue dropping everything and returning home.

"You guys know I can hear you right?" A bent over Lovina said from behind the bakery counter. The women quickly hold their tongues, unaware of how loud their counsel had been.

"Well then maybe, you should try to listen to what we are saying."

"Yes Lovina. I mean, how do you expect to-" Lovina was sure that they were still telling her how to get over how distraught and disgusted she felt, but she couldn't bear to listen to them anymore. Blocking them out, she moved back to the ovens and continued to bake alone with her thoughts.

As Lovina walked home from the bakery that night, it was hard for her not to feel the weight of her closest confidants fall on her heart. A haze still lingered over her thoughts, but Lovina was beginning to feel that something has to change. The ringing of thunder in her ears shook her from her confusion. Her eyes flash to the sky right as the clouds open up and the floodgates break. She can hear her mother's words in her ears,

"Don't run in the rain, you will only get wetter." But her reaction was unchanged. She took off through the streets that were quickly turning to mud. Her feet began to struggle to force herself through. As she takes one more larger step, Lovina falls, headfirst into the street. Feeling an almost cosmic sense of irony, Lovina can't find the will to pull herself up out of the mud.

After lying there for more time than she would care to admit to, she raised her head to see a pair of boots striding towards her. Quickly looking upon herself to adjust to prevent any scrutiny, by the time she turned her eyes back to the sky, her gaze was met with a firm hand.

"Are you alright, miss?" Lovina was at a loss for words as she gazed into his eyes. Lovina never really paid much attention to appearances, but with the man in front of her now, it was impossible to ignore. From his sharp jawline to his piercing silver eyes, Lovina had never met a man so handsome. He offers his hand once more, shaking Lovina from her state, and she takes it as he lifts her to her feet.

"Thank you, sir."

"What's a lady like you doing out here alone with no umbrella? This isn't exactly the best weather for a casual stroll." Lovina laughs as the man holds his jacket over her head.

"I was on my way home from the bakery where I work and I thought I could make it home before the rain, but I guess luck was not in my favor today." The man looked over her muddy appearance and stifled a laugh.

"Well, I am on my way home as well, is there somewhere I can take you on the way?"

"Oh no, thank you, but you don't have to do that."

"Miss, I wouldn't feel right about leaving you on your own. I mean, what would happen if you fell in the mud again?" Lovina met the man's eyes again; but this time they were sparkling.

"Well, I am headed down this road a bit further, where is your home?"

"I live down the same way. I am staying with Deacon Macon and his wife until I can finish my home."

"Alright, well if we are already heading in the same direction, I guess it would be alright for you to escort me home." The man smiled and held out his arm, which she took and they continued down the road. Though they didn't say much outside of the normal pleasantries - who they were, where they are from, and what they do - Lovina couldn't remember a time when she had felt this relaxed as she walked home. By the time they arrived at her door, it felt as if no time had passed at all.

"Thank you for escorting me. I really do appreciate the gesture. I wish I could repay you for sparing me a bit of my dignity."

"Think nothing of it. I just did what any man should do."

"Well I would still like to show my gratitude in some way... How about you come by the bakery tomorrow and you can walk me home and I can bring you some food?"

"That sounds like something I would be interested in."

"Good. I will see you tomorrow night then, Mr... I'm so sorry it seems I never got your name."

"Thomas. Thomas Elton. And you are?"

"Lovina."

"Well Miss Lovina, I will see you tomorrow night." And with the tip of his hat, he backed off of her porch, and continued down the path.

Lovina had to remind herself to breathe as she gazed at his figure disappear around the corner at the end of the lane. As she closed her door, her back thudded against it - cementing her disbelief in what she has just done. Inviting a man - not just to visit her place of work, but to walk her home for a second time. As much as she had managed to shock herself, she had to turn that emotion off in order to get herself ready for the day that was to come. She quickly cleaned herself off and hung the wet clothes out to dry before wrapping herself in a blanket and falling quickly asleep in anticipation of the day that was to come.

Chapter Two

"Lovina what are you waiting for? You have been pinning out that window all day." Cynthia couldn't understand this overnight shift in behavior. Lovina's behavior was also a shock to the ladies at the bakery. Her hair wasn't slicked back in a bun, but her auburn locks flowed over her shoulders and her face was brighter than they had seen it in months.

"What do you mean?" Lovina asked without so much as batting her eyes as her gaze continued out the window. The ladies shared looks and whispered to one another trying to pinpoint what has caused the flippant change in their friend when all of a sudden the door opened.

"I am sorry, but we are about to close-" Cynthia bit her tongue before she could finish dismissing the man now standing in the entrance. Lovina's eyes met his immediately, giving her a better look in the daylight than she got the night before. His silver eyes sparkled the same, if not more intensely with the help of the sun's rays; and his strong figure wasn't menacing, but warm and open. She also was able to get a better look at his strong jaw and ruffled copper hair and stubble that adorned his face.

"I'm sorry for my lateness."

"Oh no, you are right on time. I was just about to leave." As much as the other women wanted to take in every second of this exchange, they knew that it was not right to spy. Quickly Cynthia pushed the ladies towards the back door and excused herself in an attempt of being discreet, but in her stuttering of words and lack of ability to keep her eyes from darting from the pair, discretion was not something that she was able to achieve.

"I apologize for my aunt. She can be a bit much sometimes."

"I don't mind. She reminds me a lot of my grandmother, God rest her soul." The pair exchange a smile and Lovina grabs a box from behind the counter.

"Here you are, as I promised."

"You know, you really didn't have to go to the trouble."

"I wanted to. This is one of the few things that I seem to be good at, so let me use my skill to thank you." Thomas smiled as Lovina handed over the box. He then offered his arm and escorted her out of the building and down the lane.

Before the pair realized, this became a regular thing. Everyday at closing time, Thomas would enter the bakery - sometimes a bit dirtier than other times depending upon what his work was that day - and Lovina would be waiting for him to walk her home. This went on for almost four months before Thomas decided to be brave.

"So, I am having dinner with Deacon Macon and his wife this evening for the first time in my house."

"You finished the house? That's so exciting."

"Yes... well I was wondering if maybe you would like to join us tonight for dinner." Lovina was ecstatic to hear this question as it floated through the air. "I mean, if you already have plans don't worry about it or anything-"

"I would love to come." Thomas let a big smile spread across his face.

"Great! Dinner will be around 7. Do you want me to come and fetch you or...?"

"I can call upon the Deacon. I am sure we can all walk over together. Besides, it has been so long since I've spoken with Mrs. Macon." Thomas nodded is head in understanding, as the air now buzzed with their intertwined excitement for the evening to come.

Lovina put on her newest and cleanest dress and fixed her hair up all pretty before walking a few houses down to meet the Macons. As she walked up their path, Mrs. Macon opened the door and greeted Lovina with a warm hug.

"Lovina, dear, it's been too long."

"I agree. I am sorry I haven't been by to visit all that much."

"My dear, you never have to apologize to me for anything. You're parents did right by me, and I know that they would have approved of the decision you made, despite how difficult it was for you." Lovina's smile dropped for a moment, but Mrs. Macon felt the need to quickly amend her statement.

"What I mean to say- I mean- Under the same circumstances, I would never have been able to- to-"

"Mrs. Macon, I thought we agreed not to bring up any of those unhappy moments tonight. Especially with all of the happiness that may enter our lives after tonight." Deacon took his wife's hands and made her beautiful smile spread across her face. Deacon turns his head to Lovina, his well groomed facade couldn't hide his excitement and his overwhelming emotions for something she didn't quite understand.

"Deacon, thank you for escorting me this evening along with your wife. I know when we are together we can be a bit much."

"It is no problem at all Lovina. I know that this dinner is something Thomas has been wanting to plan since he met you. I don't know what you have done, but in the whole time I have known him, he has never been as positive or as happy as he has been since he's been courting you."

"Did he say that, did he use those words?"

"Which words?"

"Daniel Macon, do not tease the poor girl." Lovina bore holes into the older couple. Praying that the words she heard meant what she thought they meant. Deacon looked onto Lovina as his eyes answered her question without him needing to utter even one syllable. Lovina's face flushes, unable to keep her happiness from revealing itself. The Macons looked on Lovina with such love and care as they ushered her out of their home onto the street and - in their minds - into the rest of her life.

Thomas had been stressing all day. Was his house clean enough for her? Was the food he prepared good enough for her? All of these questions and more flooded through his mind until the knock came at his door. Fear ratcheting up with every step he took towards the door, he turned the knob, and then suddenly it was like everything had melted away. The instant he saw Lovina's face, all of the fears, doubts, and confusion melted away and he was blissfully happy.

The Macons felt the connection between the young couple the moment the door opened; and they couldn't have been happier. After having Thomas live with them for all those months while his house was being built, and after knowing Lovina practically her entire life, they couldn't imagine a better scenario for either of them. Deacon did - however - clear his throat after an uncomfortable amount of silence had passed.

The dinner went smoothly - much to Thomas's glee - and after some good conversation and a stroll around Thomas's property, the Macons decided to call it a night; however, Lovina decided to stay behind.

"Thank you for dinner."

"It was my pleasure, Lovina. But frankly, I feel that I owe you much more than one simple meal."

"You don't owe me anything, why do you keep saying that?"

"Because it's the truth." Lovina looked up at the man as he shuffled his feet. He seemed off somehow to her. His frame - usually so strong and firm - seemed more open and weaker in a sense. This change confused her, and she tried to meet his gaze in order to find out why his demeanor was so changed.

"Is everything alright? Did I do something wrong?"

"No! No, not at all!"

"Well then why won't you look at me? Everything was fine during dinner, but now it's like you can't even bring yourself to look at me..."

"I'm just..."

"Just what?"

"I'm afraid." Lovina nodded her head for him to explain further as to why he was so fearful. "I'm afraid of something I have been feeling and I am unsure as to how to proceed because I do not know how to discuss it with you without potentially ruining our friendship." Lovina moved across the room to him, gliding with each step, and placed her hands in his.

"Ask me. Please." Her eyes pleading for the question she had been waiting so long to receive from him. Thomas's eyes ignite as he holds her hands in his, but before he can get one word out, there is a knock at the door. Assuming that it is the Macons, Thomas yells towards the door,

"What did you forget Deacon?" A few moments of silence before the reply and then a voice spoke up that none of them expected:

"Lovina, we need to talk."

Chapter Three

Lovina was frozen. Inches from Thomas's warm embrace, the man who destroyed her world entered her gaze. She didn't know whether to laugh or cry; push Thomas away or hold him closer. Lovina's head lowered as she attempted to reign her thoughts in.

"Lovina, we need to talk?" She spat his words back at him as she turned to face him.

"I don't think you two have anything to discuss frankly." Thomas stated as he put himself between Luke and Lovina. He stood strong - however, Lovina could feel his muscles tense and hear his heartbeat quicken - as he stood as a protective barrier. Luke's gaze tore momentarily from Lovina to square off against the man in his way. He scoffed,

"And who are you to make her decisions for her?" Thomas looked upon Lovina, unsure of how to categorize their relationship to her former suitor. Lovina couldn't help but notice the stark contrasts between

"Luke, please. Now is not a good time."

"Oh! Now isn't a good time? And I suppose earlier at the diner was also a bad time?"

"Luke, I-"

"Wait, why didn't you tell me he showed up at the diner?" Thomas his voice tinged with concern, not the anger Lovina had expected. Before she could explain why she didn't tell him about her and Luke's earlier encounter, Luke decided it was a brilliant time to speak once more.

"You need to make your mind up Lovina. You can't love me but go run off anytime I'm not around."

"Run around?" Luke realized that it was too late to remove the foot from his mouth. "I never ran around on you." Lovina pushed down on Thomas's arms that were shielding her from the man who broke her spirit. "You left me for someone else simply because I wouldn't sleep with you until we were married. You threw away a four year courtship or relationship, whatever you want to call it; over pursuing the pleasures of the flesh."

"Lovina, it's not that simple."

"Of course it's that simple! When you left me, after all of my pleading and hoping and begging for you to reconsider, the only thing you told me as to why you were leaving is that I wouldn't sleep with you." Thomas's face fell as he saw the tears flowing angrily from the woman he had come to love. He makes a move to her, but Lovina's eyes flash towards him to stay exactly where he is.

"Lovina, please. Can we not have this conversation in front of-"

"I want him to hear. I need someone else to understand that I am not crazy for being as broken as I was."

"Wait... you never-"

"No. As angry as you made me and as broken as you left me, I never once shared with anyone that you left me for someone who would sleep with you."

"Why did you do that?"

"You were the golden boy of town. What would have happened if I slandered your name? I would have lost my credibility and I would be scorned for the town only loved me because they loved you." Luke's mind was swimming. At the time, he was convinced he was making the right decision, but now as he stood in front of the woman he left behind, and his once confident thoughts began to waiver. Thomas sees Luke's hesitation and takes what he believes to be his last chance. Moving once more into Lovina's bubble, he pushes the hair out of her face and tilts her chin to meet his gaze.

"Just say the word. Whatever you want from me, I'm here." His strong hands rest on her cheeks. Placing her hands on top of his, Lovina stroked his long fingers and saw herself in the reflection of his mirror like eyes. The image she saw shocked her. After months of being told that she had become gaunt and pale in coloring, the woman she saw in his eyes was strong and healthy.

"So that's how you see me."

"You are so much more to me than your shell. You always have been." Lovina's vision became blurry - as for the first time in she couldn't remember how long - she was crying for a reason other than sadness. Her hands, unbeknownst to her, rested on his chest before she circled them around his neck as she drew herself into him. As she sniffled into his shirt, Lovina began to take in every aspect of this moment. From the musty smell of wood from the shop to his strong arms holding her against him, making her feel that he would become her new foundation. As a smile spreads across her face, Lovina hears Luke clear his throat.

"Excuse me, but I would prefer if you removed your hands from my girl."

"What, so because she once agreed to marry you she was supposed to just sit around here pinning after you despite the fact that you skipped town for someone outside our way of life?" Luke's eyes flash to Lovina.

"How dare you tell a stranger about my personal business! I thought you were different!"

"ME?" Lovina's blood boiled in her veins as Luke tossed his accusations around the room. "You destroyed my life. You made a commitment to me, my parents - God rest their souls - and then just because you weren't happy with my opinions on the sanctity of marriage, you left."

"Well all of that is behind us now, we can move on together and grow back together. I never loved her like I love you; not even close."

"Then why did you leave me?" Lovina took four strong steps towards the man making her blood boil and her eyes overflow. "If you claim to love me so much, how could you have barred to leave me? Even if you couldn't overcome your sinful desires - or your human instincts as you will argue they were - why didn't you come back after you had been satisfied and begged my forgiveness?"

"Come on darling-"

"You don't get to call me that. You will address me properly if you wish to address me at all."

"Why are you being so stubborn? Women would kill for a man like me to offer you what I'm offering."

"What exactly are you offering her?" Thomas decided to re enter the drama unfolding in her living space. Luke's face hardened as his eyes shifted from Lovina to Thomas.

"I'm offering her a life; and a good one at that. I am a successful businessman and have plenty of money to where she can quit that stupid bakery job and come stay at home so we can start raising a family. Lovina has always wanted a family and I am prepared to provide her with that."

"I may want a family; but you of all people should know that bakery means everything to me." Lovina shocked both herself and the two men stood across from her with her outburst.

"Lovina-"

"I'm alright, Thomas." Lovina shares a sweet smile with Thomas before returning her gaze to Luke. "Let me make this as crystal clear as I possibly can: yes, I did once love you; but now you have made it impossible for me to ever forgive you. I may not have been able to see then because I was blinded by love, but you never actually learned anything about me. You don't know about why I love the bakery so much, and you will never understand why I can't forgive you for why you left."

"Are you sure this is the choice you want to make? You are choosing a hired hand over a business owner. You will never be wealthy."

"I don't need to be wealthy. After all of this time, I finally understand what it is that I have been looking so long for: I need to and I deserve to be happy." Turning to Thomas, her eyes shed their last tear. "And Thomas makes me irrevocably happy." Thomas strides over to her as her words hit his ears. He threw his arms around her waist and hoists her up and spins her around. The loving pair embraced as Luke, ashamed and embarrassed, was left to hang his head in shame as he slipped out her door.

Chapter Four

The weeks after the toxicity of her last relationship walked out of her life - and clear out of town - flew by. Though they claimed they weren't rushing things, Lovina and Thomas could barely contain their desire to get married. Before they knew it, the day arrived and people were entering the church. Lovina waited in the bridal chamber, awaiting her aunt to retrieve her. It wasn't a large room, but it was clean and pretty. Something you would imagine would have a likeness to a Victorian sitting room. Lovina smoothed the lines in her skirt down as took a turn around the room. There was a loveseat or fainting couch - it wasn't very large to say the least - two chairs, and a small table. Lovina walked around the room twice before resting upon the couch. As she can't help but smile to herself, Lovina is awoken from her trance by a knock at her door.

"Who is it?"

"It's Deacon Macon, Lovina. May I come in for a moment?"

"Of course," Lovina strides to the door to open it. "What's going on? He's not backing out is he?" Now fearing that she has lost out once again.

"Oh no, nothing of the sort." To that Lovina could breathe a sigh of relief. "I am just here to pass along a message from the groom. Apparently he doesn't think he will have occasion to tell you everything he wants to today and - because he doesn't want to forget - he wrote it down here for you." Deacon Macon extended his hand that held a folded cream piece of paper. Lovina laughed to herself realizing Thomas must have used one of her recipe sheets from the bakery. Taking the paper from Deacon Macon, he bowed out gracefully and left her alone. She sat back down on the loveseat by the window and unfolded the paper before she began to read.

My dearest Lovina,

This is the happiest day of my life. You have done more for me in these few months than I have been able to do for myself in my whole life. I am writing this short dictation to you because I need you to know exactly how I feel if I am unable to speak after I see you walk through the door in mere moments.

I know that we met at a time when you were not feeling like you would ever be happy again, and I want to make sure that you are sure that I am the one who will make you happy forever. I understand at times you may not trust me, you may question me, and you may even be mad at me for something I may not understand. Despite this however, I want you to know that I will not be mad. I will not meet your anger with violence, and I will NOT shame you for feelings you have every right to feel because of how you have been wronged.

I don't mean to bring up unhappy memories on our happy day, but I need you to know that I love you unconditionally, irrevocably, and entirely. I have never felt the kind of love I feel for you, and I can only attest that God must have made me for you and you for me. The only thing I could pray to ask him would be for us to have met sooner so we could have started our life together sooner.

Now, with all that out of the way, this is what I promise to you:

I promise to always love and be with only you.

I promise that whatever children we have, I will love and cherish as much as you.

I promise to raise our children in our faith and our culture to cement their knowledge of our ways.

I promise to take care of my family for as long as I live and even after if I leave before my time.

I promise not to be out late and to help you around the house when I am able.

No matter how old or how weak we grow, I will never leave your side.

Finally, I promise that once a day at least, I will tell you I love you. It may not always be verbally, but whether through a look, through a nod, or an embrace, you will know everyday of our lives together how much I love and will always love you.

Well, I am sure there is more that I am leaving out, but you know I am not very good at typing up a conversation or a letter for that matter... I can't wait to see you and I can't wait to call you my wife.

I love you.

Yours.

Lovina held back tears as she let her hand fall upon her lap. She took her fingers and ran them along the words he wrote to her. Thomas was giving her more than he would ever know, and this note solidifies to her that she will need to make sure she tells him this much and more about how much he means to her.

Life is never simple, nor is it patient and kind. But when you have someone to walk along beside you on this crazy journey, it becomes a bit easier. It isn't an immediate thing, it takes time and effort; but if you are willing to put in the work, someone else will be willing to as well.

AMISH AGAINST THE ODDS

Monica Marks

59

There was a slight buzzing in her ears but it had been there for the better part of two weeks, something Rachel had grown accustomed to hearing. She knew it wasn't medical but it alarmed her all the same.

It does not take a doctor to see I am blocking outside noise in my own way, she thought ruefully.

It wasn't until Joanna tugged gently on her skirt that she realized someone was trying to get her attention.

"*Mammi*? Bishop Bachman is summoning you."

Rachel glanced down at her small daughter and offered her a quick smile.

"Oh."

She looked toward where Joanna pointed and indeed, the Bishop was waving almost comically for her to join him.

"Come along, *liebchen*," she said to the six-year-old and Joanna followed closely on her mother's heels.

"Lovely service, Bishop," Rachel told the elder without preamble. She did not want to give him a chance to open with platitudes.

He nodded appreciatively and patted Joanna on the head endearingly.

"Did you enjoy it also, little Jo?"

Rachel cringed inwardly, hoping her outspoken child would have something nice to say and to her relief, Joanna nodded eagerly.

"Yes, Bishop Bachman. I like listening to you speak about forgiveness and repentance."

Rachel exhaled slowly, hardly realizing she had been holding her breath.

"They are lessons which we must never forget, regardless of how difficult a time we encounter, right Jo?"

"Yes, Bishop," the child agreed and Rachel tried to ignore the obvious message the Bishop had delivered to her specifically.

"Very good, Jo. Off you go then. I would like to speak with your mother alone."

Rachel stifled a groan. She had intentionally brought Joanna along in hopes that she would not be left to hear the bishop's words of wisdom that afternoon.

"Walk along side me, Rachel," the Bishop ordered and Rachel idly wondered what would happen if she politely refused. It was a fleeting thought, a wicked fantasy rather than something she was apt to do.

She loved Bishop Bachman well. He was a decent man and strong leader. That did not mean she wished to be subjected to his well-meaning advice.

"Of course," she agreed and they headed away from the congregation toward the pond in the middle of the Troyer farm.

"How are you faring these days, Rachel?"

She inadvertently gritted her teeth together and the bishop seemed to catch her expression before she could hide it.

"Rachel, I know this is a trying time for you but I want you to understand you are not alone."

She nodded, trying to force a cheerful smile onto her face but she was certain she was about to dissolve into a puddle of tears if he continued to press her.

"I know," she replied. "I am blessed to have the support of my family and the district."

Bishop Bachman stopped walking and turned to regard her.

"And the Umbels?"

The familiar lump formed quickly, barely giving Rachel enough time to swallow her misery.

She shook her head.

"I do not see much of them but in casual passing," she confessed. The bishop sighed regretfully, his eyes moving toward her in-laws who tried not to stare back at them in the distance. Bishop Bachman returned his gaze to Rachel.

"That is unfortunate but you must understand they feel as badly as you do. It will take time to heal but everyone will get there, *Gotte* willing."

Rachel did not answer, her own eyes shifting back toward where her daughter tagged along after some older children. She purposely avoided looking at the Umbels.

"You already know that your focus must be on Joanna and she seems to be thriving despite the circumstances."

Rachel nodded, her fingers reaching up to play with a strand of honey-blonde hair. It was a nervous habit she had forsaken years earlier but it seemed to have resurfaced in the past weeks.

"Who is helping you on the farm?"

Rachel wondered why he asked questions he already knew the answer to but she dared not voice her own inquiry.

He does not mean any harm. You must not lose your temper with the Bishop.

"I am faring just fine," she fibbed, returning her stare to his concerned eyes. She forced a tight smile onto her lips.

"It is not a big farm, Bishop and I really do not need much to keep it going. Most of my income is from my quilts these days. The farm is secondary."

"Be that as it may, Rachel, you should not be tending to it alone. I will see about having someone help you."

She opened her mouth to protest.

The last thing she wanted was another neighbor prying into the intimate and embarrassing details of what had happened with Eli.

It is not as if they do not already know. They likely knew before I did, she thought bitterly. All Rachel wanted to do was disappear into a world with her daughter and forget the rest of the community.

Overnight it seemed, the life she had cherished in the close-knit Amish district had become a place of alienation and isolation.

The people she had once wanted to share her life with became those to avoid.

"Rachel?" the Bishop pressed. "Will you allow me to find you help?"

She knew there would be no point in arguing with the man. His intentions were good and she knew his worry was genuine.

"That will be fine," she replied. "I should get back to Joanna."

He nodded although Rachel could tell he did not consider the conversation finished.

It is not the last I have heard of this, she thought, sighing silently. *I wonder if I will ever hear the last of this.*

"Hello."

Samuel looked up from the fence post and did a double take as he saw the man standing a few feet away.

"Hello," Samuel replied, rising to his full height. He dropped the hammer in his tool belt and cocked his head to the side, peering at the stranger. He brushed a strand of light brown hair from his face and stared inquisitively at the man.

"Do you work for hire or are you employed by this farmer?"

Samuel's brown eyes narrowed suspiciously.

"I would ask if you were from the IRS but something tells me you aren't," he replied, a slightly sarcastic tone lacing his words.

The stranger chuckled and extended a hand.

"No, you would be correct. I am not from the IRS. My name is Mark Bachman. I am a Bishop with the Amish district just that way. You are?"

Samuel eyed his outstretched palm reluctantly but stepped forward to accept it.

"Samuel Baker."

"Good to meet you, Mr. Baker. I have a member of our district who needs some help on her farm. She has the unfortunate task of tending the land herself, something that happened quite recently. Is this something which might interest you?"

Samuel withdrew his hand and stepped back, his brow knitting in consternation.

"Don't you people help your own?" he asked gruffly. The Bishop seemed amused by his question.

"We try to," he replied. "But sometimes we need outsider assistance. Of course, you would be compensated well for your efforts."

Samuel looked around, wiping the sweat from his neck. He stared at the Bishop, considering the man's words.

Work had been sparse and he had bills to pay. Samuel knew he would be foolish to turn down an offer like that but he could not help but feel suspicious of this bizarre chance encounter.

"How did you come across me?" Samuel demanded. Bishop Bachman pointed at his wagon just down the dirt road.

"I happened to be driving by and I saw you. I have just finished services and I am returning to my home. Truth be told, I think you were a sign from God. I was going to begin looking for help for Rachel in the morning but here you are, working on a Sunday."

Samuel nodded slowly.

"Unfortunately, my bills don't understand days of the week," he muttered and the elder laughed aloud.

"It is one of the many trials and tribulations the English face, I fear. If you were to accept my proposal, you would have Sundays as a day of rest."

Samuel tried to remember a time when any day had been a day of rest.

I haven't rested in years.

So what do you say? Would you be willing to help Rachel on her farm?"

"Is it steady work?"

Samuel wondered why he bothered voicing the question; he was already going to take the job, steady work or not.

"Yes, it is," Bishop Bachman replied. "My guess is for as long as you're willing to do it."

Samuel nodded.

"When does it start?"

"You can begin tomorrow if you are available."

Sam grinned for the first time since meeting the Amish man and extended his palm again.

"I'm available."

"*Mammi*, where did *Daed* go?"

It was not the first time which Joanna had asked the question but it never ceased to send a thousand needles into Rachel's heart.

"Joanna, what have I told you about your father?" she replied, grinding her jaw.

"He has gone away," the child chirped. "But where? And when will he return?"

"He is not coming back!" Rachel's voice was much harsher than she had intended and a look of hurt crossed over her face.

"I am sorry, *Mammi*," she whispered and Rachel was instantly filled with shame.

She is only a child, longing for her father! You have no cause to snap at her like that!

Rachel extended her arms.

"No, *liebchen*, I am sorry," she gasped, tears springing to her green eyes. "Come here."

Dutifully, Joanna ran into her mother's arms and the two embraced.

"*Daed* is not coming back, not ever," she breathed. "I am sorry to tell you that but you must stop asking about him."

"Why *Mammi*? Why can I not ask about him?"

Rachel bit on her lower lip and buried her face in Joanna's soft blonde mop of hair.

"You must go now, Jo. You will be late for school."

They parted and Jo looked up at her mother.

"Why are you crying, *Mammi*?"

"I only have something in my eye," she fibbed. "Off you go now."

Begrudgingly, Joanna trudged toward the door, glancing back at her mother one last time. Rachel waved encouragingly and painted a smile upon her face.

She is too young to understand any of this. How can I explain it when I barely understand myself.

Rachel sighed and turned back to the sink where she was doing the breakfast dishes.

She had a mountain of work to accomplish that day and she did not know if she would get half of it done. She recalled her conversation with Bishop Bachman the previous day.

I shouldn't be so head strong. I do need help and I should get some assistance before I lose control of the farm. It has only been two weeks and things are already becoming overwhelming.

Rachel reluctantly realized she would be forced to ask her family for help but she knew with their help came an earful of unsolicited advice.

A knock at the front door shattered her thoughts and she glanced back to see Bishop Bachman on the porch.

She waved him inside, drying her hands on her apron.

Ah, speaking of unsolicited advice...

She was immediately filled with contrition.

You should be grateful he cares enough about you to see if you are well.

"*Guder mariye*, Rachel," he called as he entered the small house.

"*Guder mariye*," she replied. "To what do I owe the pleasure, Bishop?"

She hoped he was not about to speak to her about Eli again.

"I have someone whom I would like you to meet," he said as she moved to join him at the entranceway.

Rachel's eyebrows shot up to her hairline.

He cannot mean...

Instantly, Bishop Bachman seemed to read the look of dread on her face.

"It is a handyman," he said quickly and Rachel was filled with a relief so strong, it almost knocked her to her knees.

Of course he would not bring a suitor to my door so soon. Why am I looking at everyone like an enemy?

"Already you have found a handyman?" she replied, surprised. "You must have had someone in mind."

They moved toward the door and the Bishop shook his head.

"No, actually I chanced upon him on the way home yesterday."

As they stepped onto the veranda, Rachel started in shock.

"Rachel Umbel, this is Samuel Baker."

Rachel recovered from her initial reaction immediately stuck her hand out.

"Ah, thank you for coming to my assistance, Mr. Baker," she said quickly, shifting her eyes away from his face.

"No problem," he replied gruffly and Rachel wondered if he had noticed her reaction. They shook hands quickly.

"Tell me where you want me to go," he said without hesitation and Rachel could sense he was not the conversational type. She found the realization heartwarming.

I will not be forced to entertain him or answer questions all day long, she thought with some happiness.

"Do you have any experience in working with animals? The horses need grooming."

Samuel nodded and looked around, spotting the barn.

Without another word, he disappeared toward the stables, leaving the Bishop and Rachel alone.

"Who is he?" Rachel asked when he was out of earshot. "I have never seen him around the district before."

"As I said, I only just chanced upon him yesterday."

Rachel gnawed on her lower lip, debating whether to ask the obvious question or not.

"What happened to his face?" she finally whispered, her curiosity winning out. The Bishop shrugged.

"I did not think to ask," he replied nonchalantly, turning to leave. "I will be back to pick him up at four o'clock."

Rachel nodded, watching at the Bishop got onto his wagon.

He did not think to ask how that man's face got so horribly disfigured? She thought, shaking her head. *How could he not wish to know?*

Rachel forced the thought of Samuel from her mind and began addressing her long list of chores.

She had her own issues to worry about without bringing in an Englisher's problems also.

Maybe it is time to go back to the city, he thought. *Work is too scarce in Amish country and even if this is steady income, I don't belong here.*

Samuel wondered if he belonged anywhere anymore.

It had been five years since he had called any place "home", wandering from town to town like a nomad. He had no friends, no ties and no money.

At least I will have a better shot of employment in Detroit.

Branch County had been kind to him given his appearance but the thought of returning to the city filled him with a sick which never truly left him.

There was too great a chance he would see Holly in Detroit, no matter where he went.

Detroit has a population of third quarters of a million people. You will not see Holly.

He tried to shove the thought of her from his mind but it seemed her anguished face would forever be etched there.

Maybe in another year, he thought, blinking quickly against his burning lids. *Maybe then I will be able to return to Detroit and face what I have done.*

But he didn't believe himself. It was the same thing he told himself every year around the time of the anniversary.

Sam knew that the pain did not go away, no matter how much he avoided contact with others or hid himself away in the boonies.

It wouldn't happen next near.

He would never go home because home did not exist for him anymore.

The late afternoon sun filtered into the front room and Rachel glanced up suddenly, blinking. She peered down at the quilt she had been sewing and then at the clock in the corner of the room.

How long have I been in here? She thought in shock. She had worked through lunch and her fingers were throbbing.

She had wanted to finish the piece for sale at market on Friday but she had not meant to spend a great deal of time on it, not when there was so much else to be done before Joanna returned from school.

She rose from the rocking chair and peered out the window into the front yard.

And what happened to the Englisher?

A spark of anger coursed through her as she threw open the front door, slightly blinded by the rays. She had not seen him since first thing that morning when she had sent him to groom the horses.

He is probably taking a nap. Why did I agree to let the Bishop bring someone here?

Angrily, she hurried around the back of the house toward the barn and threw open the doors, freezing in her tracks.

The two horses were gleaming and well-groomed in spotless stalls with fresh hay. Samuel had swept out the interior and maintained the unoccupied booths also.

Rachel was sure she had never seen the stables so clean.

She was immediately ashamed for thinking the worst of the Englisher and she looked around to see where he had gone.

If he is napping, he has certainly earned a rest, she thought wryly. *This is more than Eli could accomplish in a day.*

She found Samuel in the garden, weeding through the tomato plants, sweat glistening on his neck and shoulders. There was no sweat on his scarred face and Rachel wondered if he was in constant pain. She certainly hoped not.

She watched him for a moment, touched by his work ethic. No one had guided him to the garden; he had simply taken the task upon himself as he had cleaning out the barn.

"You did good work with the horses," she called out to him. He barely raised his head but he nodded slightly to acknowledge her words.

"Have you taken any water or eaten yet?"

Samuel paused and glanced at her for a moment, seeming unsure of himself. Rachel was struck at how bright brown his eyes seemed through his mangled face and yet she did not find looking at him as unsettling as she had earlier.

Despite his exterior, Rachel could sense a gentleness beneath him, one he seemed to want to keep hidden.

"No, I am fine," he finally answered, turning back to the plants.

"I cannot have you fainting in the sun," Rachel insisted sternly. "Please come in the house for some water at least."

He paused and Rachel reasoned his thirst must have won out in the end.

"All right," he agreed but Rachel thought she heard a slight resentment in his tone.

Silently, he followed her back toward the house and into the side door.

In the kitchen, they didn't speak as Rachel fixed him a glass of lemonade. As she placed the glass before him, she thought he was about to protest but he shut his mouth and took a long sip.

Rachel turned back to the refrigerator.

"I will fix us some lunch," she announced.

"No thank you," Samuel answered quickly. "I should get back to work."

She glanced at him over her shoulder and shook her head.

"You have accomplished more today than I had expected to do all week," she replied. "You can take time for lunch."

Samuel was silent but she could feel him watching her as she made a plate of cheese, bread and fruit.

She set the plate at the table and joined him.

"Do you believe in God?" she asked, glancing at him as he reached for his food. He seemed taken aback by the question.

"I used to," he replied, ripping off a hunk of bread with surprisingly straight teeth. "But he doesn't seem to come around much for me these days."

Rachel nodded and bowed her head.

"Thank you, *Gotte* for sending me help when I needed it most. Please bless our food. Amen."

Samuel dropped his bread and looked embarrassed.

"Amen," he echoed quickly. "I'm sorry. It didn't occur to me to pray."

Rachel smiled and began to eat.

"There is no need to apologize. You are entitled to your beliefs. I did not wish to exclude you if you wished to join," she explained.

Samuel chewed on his morsels slowly, studying her furtively and Rachel sensed that he wanted to say something.

You invited him in to eat. You should encourage him to speak, she thought but in truth, she was rather enjoying the silence of someone who knew nothing about her or her past.

"Did your husband die recently?"

The question was blunt and caught Rachel off guard. She stared at him with clear green eyes, her mouth slightly agape.

Her first instinct was indignation but suddenly, she began to laugh.

"In a way," she replied and Samuel stared at her, his brow raised in surprise at her odd reaction. He did not question her further.

"I am sorry for your loss," he muttered, fixating his eyes on the table. "It is not easy to lose someone you love."

Rachel was moved by his tone and despite her resolve not to engage in conversation, she found herself intrigued by the hardworking stranger.

"Are you married?" she asked.

"Not anymore."

He is as vague as I am, she thought, partly amused, partly annoyed. She wondered if he was simply treating her the way she was treating him.

Do unto others...

"You are very good around the farm," she told him. "Do you have a farm of your own?"

He shook his head.

"No," he replied. "I grew up on one though, before I moved to Michigan."

The sound of hooves approaching the house caused them to glance out of the window and suddenly Rachel saw Joanna skip around the side of the property.

"My daughter is home," she said, rising and dusting the crumbs from her apron as Joanna came slipping through the door. "But I can't see who has come by wagon."

"*Mammi*, Bishop Bachman is - "

Joanna turned to stone as she took in the stranger in her kitchen. Her small face became a mask of fear as she stared at Samuel, her mouth open with fear.

Terrified that Joanna would say something impolite, Rachel piped up immediately.

"Joanna, this is Mr. Baker. He will be helping us on the farm. Samuel, this is my daughter Joanna."

She nudged her daughter gently but Joanna could not seem to overcome her horror of Samuel's scarred face and hid her eyes in her mother's skirt.

Rachel turned apologetically to Samuel.

"I am sorry," she started. "She's shy – "

It was at that moment that she realized Samuel's face was a statue still as Joanna's had been. He gaped at the girl, his fierce eyes wide with an emotion Rachel could not place.

"Samuel, are you all right?" Rachel asked.

"Hello? Rachel? Are you here?" Bishop Bachman called, entering the house through the front door. The elder's voice seemed to shatter Samuel's trance-like state.

"I didn't know you had a daughter," Samuel mumbled, spinning to leave. "I – I'm sorry. I can't come back here."

He disappeared from the kitchen, almost barreling over Bishop Bachman who appeared in the doorway. The bishop's smile faded as he watched Samuel run out the door toward his wagon.

"What happened? Did it go badly today?" he demanded but Rachel had no answer for him.

She pulled Joanna close to her, her heart racing.

"*Mammi,* is that man a monster?" Joanna whispered.

"Dear *Gotte*, I hope not, *liebchen*," Rachel murmured in response.

The fire raged hot and terrifying. Joanna's screams could scarcely be heard above the popping of the wood beams and Rachel raced about looking for her daughter.

"Joanna!" she cried, tears streaking down her face. "Joanna, where are you?"

But the child only continued to shriek and Rachel tried to find her despite the billowing, blinding smoke encasing the barn.

She saw a movement out of the corner of her eye and suddenly, Samuel emerged, holding Joanna, limp in his arms, his eyes wild.

Rachel began to howl.

Rachel started awake, her body drenched in sweat.

Without hesitation, she slipped from her bed and rushed into Joanna's room, pushing open the door in fear.

The child lay sleeping peacefully, her body half curled with a soft smile on her face.

Slowly, Rachel's breath steadied but she could not bring herself to leave the room and she slid quietly onto the single mattress beside her daughter.

She could not forget the crazed expression in Samuel's eyes from her dream.

Who did I allow into my house? She thought, willing herself to be calm.

It did not matter; he would not be back.

For some inexplicable reason, the reality of that filled Rachel with sadness.

As dawn broke, Rachel had not slept again and reluctantly she left Joanna's side to make breakfast.

There was a darkness to the day and Rachel sensed they were in for rain.

It will be a good day to work on my quilts, she thought and immediately she was grateful for the work that Samuel had done on the farm the previous day. Losing a day to bad weather was something she could not afford in her position.

Confusion filled her.

How can I be thankful he helped and fear him also?

She was beginning to wonder if the dream had not been a warning but something else.

It is irrelevant now. Samuel is gone and you must find someone else to help on the farm.

Sighing, she continued to fix the morning meal and Joanna eventually slipped downstairs.

"*Guder mariye, Mammi,*" the child chirped, slipping onto a chair.

"Hello, *liebchen*. Did you sleep well?"

Joanna nodded.

"I had a wonderful dream," she told her mother, her bright green eyes wide.

"What did you dream of?"

"The Englisher from yesterday," she replied and Rachel stared at her in shock.

"What of him?" she demanded, her face growing hot with worry.

"He brought me to a field with flowers, all with many colors and tall grasses. There was another little girl there too. He told me her name was Brittany. She and I skipped and played, picking flowers and praying together. And you know what *Mammi*?"

Unexpected tears filled Rachel's eyes.

"What, Jo?"

"The Englisher's face was not scarred. He was pleasant to look at."

Rachel's voice caught in her throat.

We both dreamt of him last night but very different dreams. I wonder what it means.

"Eat your breakfast, *liebchen*."

Joanna nodded agreeably, leaving Joanna to her thoughts.

Samuel lay on his bed, unable to move as memories consumed him, filling him with devastation and pain.

I reacted very badly yesterday, he thought, his heart heavy but he could not bring himself to move. *I will never be able to overcome this. I will be haunted by Brittany and Holly until I die.*

Seeing Joanna Umbel had stirred something in him which he had tried to suppress for years but he should have known it would rear its ugly head at the most inopportune time.

Now I have alarmed Rachel and ruined the only chance I have had for steady employment in such a long time.

There was more to it, something Samuel did not want to admit to himself.

He was strangely drawn to Rachel, despite her somewhat standoffish nature.

Maybe that is why I am drawn to her, he reasoned. *She is not pushy or intrusive. She leaves me alone but she seems caring. I wonder what happened to her husband.*

There was a knock on the door to his basement apartment and Samuel made no move to answer it.

"Samuel? It's Bishop Bachman."

Sam groaned inwardly, cursing himself for allowing the bishop to know where he lived.

"Bishop, I thought I told you I'm not going back to the Umbel farm," he yelled from his spot on his cot.

"Yes, but I would like to speak with you for a moment. Please, Samuel, it's raining outside."

Sam rolled his eyes but reluctantly rose to let the older man inside.

It wasn't very godly to leave him standing in the water after all.

"Come in," he muttered begrudgingly, stepping aside for Bishop Bachman to enter. The elder removed his hat, droplets of water falling to the entranceway. He looked at Samuel apologetically.

"I am sorry to bother you so early, Samuel but I wanted to stop by and see if you had changed your mind."

Sam shook his head quickly.

"No," he replied flatly. "But thanks for checking in."

"May I ask what happened?"

Sam peered at him questioningly.

"Are you people always like this?"

The bishop seemed genuinely tickled even though Samuel had meant to sound gruff.

"If you mean do we always take care of one another then the answer is yes."

A foreign pang of appreciation sparked through Sam as he stared at the man.

"I am going to be frank with you, Samuel. Rachel is going through a very difficult time. Her husband shamed her family and the community by leaving with another woman. He has been shunned and it is not something that we take lightly. Unfortunately, Rachel has found herself feeling isolated also. She does not wish to seek counsel and I cannot say that I am surprised she has retreated into herself. I have grown concerned for her."

Samuel was shocked by the revelation.

What kind of idiot leaves a woman like that? He thought angrily. His mind went to Joanna and he swallowed a lump in his throat.

What kind of man leaves behind a beautiful daughter when he is so blessed to have one?

"When I saw you working the other day, I got the impression that you, too, enjoy your solitude. Am I mistaken?" Bishop Bachman continued.

Sam chuckled somewhat mirthlessly.

"As a rule, yes," he replied. The bishop nodded understandingly.

"I felt that your presence might be beneficial to Rachel, both from a work standpoint but also as a silent support to her. Honestly, I am surprised that you two did not get along better."

Samuel did not respond but suddenly the Bishop's unexpected approach made sense.

He saw a damaged man and he matched me with a damaged woman.

Samuel was unsure how to feel about it.

"I will not keep you, Samuel but if you should happen to change your mind, I am certain that Rachel could still use the assistance...and the companionship."

Bishop Bachman turned to leave.

"Wait a minute," Sam called after him. "I thought you Amish didn't like outsiders."

The older man turned to smile enigmatically.

"Perhaps you will not always be an outsider, Samuel. Perhaps there is a place for you in this world with us."

The idea was stunning and he watched the Bishop replace his hat, disappearing into the rain.

Did he just suggest that I join the Amish? That is crazy.

But long after Bishop Bachman left, Samuel could not shake the spark of hope which had been ignited in his belly.

How long had it been since he belonged somewhere?

The buzzing in her ears was louder than usual that morning and it did not seem to lessen no matter how Rachel tried to distract herself.

Suddenly, it seemed accompanied by a roar and her heart racing, she wondered if there was something terribly wrong.

It was not until she peered out the front window did she realize that an auto had pulled up to the farm.

Her jaw dropped suddenly as she recognized Samuel jump from the driver's seat and hurry through the rain toward the door.

Joanna had already left for school and Rachel was alone in the house, working on her quilt.

What is he doing here? She wondered but there was no fear in his arrival. If anything, she felt a slight excitement.

"Did you forget something?" she asked, staring at him quizzically as stepped onto the front porch.

"Yes," he replied. "I forgot my manners."

She eyed him in confusion.

"Your manners?" she echoed. He shrugged sheepishly and Rachel realized that he was wet despite the short distance from the car to the door.

"Come in," she urged. "I will make coffee."

Am I making a mistake allowing him inside? She wondered but in her heart, she could not reconcile Samuel Baker with darkness.

He was a man in pain, that much was clear but why?

"Thanks," he told her, sitting at the kitchen table. "Listen, I thought about it and I know I probably scared you when I left yesterday."

Rachel glanced at him.

"It was abrupt, yes," she replied diplomatically. She did not tell him about her nightmare even though it had been plaguing her all day.

"I owe you an explanation," he said.

She placed two cups of coffee on the table, offering cream and sugar before sitting across from him, ready to listen.

He stared at her for a long moment and Rachel could sense that he was gathering his courage to put the words together.

Exhaling, he started.

"Once, a long time ago, I had a successful landscaping company in Detroit. I had clients in the suburbs and I did very well. I was married. My wife's name was Holly and we had a daughter."

Rachel felt her heart begin to race as she studied his face.

"One night, I came home from work, exhausted. Holly wanted to go out with friends and she left me alone with our daughter. I put her to bed and made myself something to eat."

Samuel stopped talking, his voice choked with emotion.

"I must have fallen asleep because when I opened my eyes, the house was on fire. Flames were licking my face but all I could think about was my baby girl. I raced toward the stairs, unaware of the burns and the blisters..."

Rachel's hand flew to her mouth and she gasped.

"There were no stairs left. There was no way to the second floor. The firefighters dragged me from the house, screaming in pain but not from the charred flesh. Holly stood in the night, staring at me and I will never forget the look on her face."

Samuel hung his head. Rachel could see him visibly shaking.

"She never forgave me. How could she? Brittany was dead because of me."

"It was an accident," Rachel murmured. "You did everything you could."

Samuel shook his head.

"No, I didn't. I couldn't take the aftermath. The guilt ate me alive. I filed for a divorce even though Holly needed me to mourn the loss of our daughter. I ran and I could never go back."

Rachel could not stop the tears from falling down her cheeks, trying to imagine the loss of her child.

"How can anyone be expected to handle such a situation well?" she asked quietly. Samuel laughed shortly.

"I heard she has remarried and had another child since. She has moved on. It seems I am the only one stuck in limbo."

Suddenly Rachel remembered Joanna's dream.

"Joanna dreamt about Brittany last night," she whispered. Samuel's head jerked up and his eyes narrowed slightly.

"Is that supposed to make me feel better?"

Rachel shook her head quickly, growing excited.

"No, she did. She told me the little girl in her dream was named Brittany and she saw you before the accident."

Samuel regarded her.

"Maybe Bishop Bachman was right," he mumbled, looking at his hands in embarrassment.

"What did he say?" she asked curiously.

"He thinks that God brought us together."

Their eyes met and a slow smile formed on Rachel's mouth.

"Please never repeat this to him," she whispered, taking Samuel's hand. "But Bishop Bachman is rarely wrong."

Samuel squeezed her palm gently.

"I look forward to learning that for myself," he replied.

As if his words were the anecdote, the humming in Rachel's ears subsided.

She could hear clearly again.

HANNAH'S DILEMMA

82

ELIZA BAKER

Part One:

"Two more are gone."

Hannah King kept her eyes trained on the dough she was kneading on the butcher block counter in front of her. Her daed spoke in a low voice to her maemm as the two stood by the back door, and Hannah knew that they didn't want her to hear what they were saying. But she couldn't help but eavesdrop. She knew that they were talking about two more cows being gone. That made it the fourth theft in less than a month.

At first it had only been one cow here or there. No one had noticed at first, but when her daed's prize bull went missing, the family realized that something was wrong. Other families in the neighborhood had also been struck. The men were still trying to figure out how to catch the thief or thieves, but whoever was responsible seemed to be two steps ahead.

"No," Hannah's maemm gasped. "How can this be, Richard?"

Glancing over her shoulder, Hannah saw her daed shrug. The weariness on his face made Hannah's heart break. Who could be doing this to them? She had to believe that it was an Englischer who had a grudge against her family or the community in general. It certainly couldn't be one of their own people. That was absurd.

Hannah looked back to her bread dough before either of her parents caught her watching them. She didn't want to make them feel worse than they already did. Without their prize bull, they needed to raise the money to buy a new one. And Hannah had no idea how that would happen. Normally they would ask the bishop of their church district to dip into the community fund to help them out, but so many people had been hit by the thieves that there wouldn't be enough money to help everyone. Besides, Hannah was fairly certain that her parents didn't want to take money that others needed more.

When her maemm gave a shuddering sigh, Hannah decided that once the bread was rising, she was going to take a prayer walk. She had taken to praying while she took her daily walk, and now she craved the time alone with the Lord. Today she needed the time more than ever because she had a specific prayer request to make: she needed to find a way to help her family.

A moment later her maemm joined her back at the butcher block counter. Hannah glanced up at her quickly, and she could see that her mother had been crying. She was still trying to hold back the tears. Hannah knew that her maemm wasn't going to share with her, so she bit back her questions.

With a final roll of the dough, Hannah was satisfied that she had kneaded the bread thoroughly enough. "Maemm?" she asked. "Would you mind if I went for a walk? I'll be back in plenty of time to finish the bread for supper."

"What? Oh, *da,* of course you can go. Enjoy the nice weather." Her maemm didn't even look up from the vegetables she was chopping as she waved Hannah out of the house.

Hannah washed her hands at the pump sink, straightened her kapp, and hurried out the back door. She saw her daed and her brothers in a circle over by the barn, and she knew that he was telling them about the most recent theft. Her heart cramped in her chest, and she turned away to hurry toward her path in the woods that bordered her family's farm.

Lord, Hannah prayed, *I don't know why this is our cross to bear at the moment, but it is. I can accept that I can't have all the answers right now, but we need your help, Lord. How can I help my family earn more money so that we can replace the livestock that we have lost? How do I convince my parents to let me help? I'm listening, Lord. Amen.*

Wind rustled the leaves of the trees, so Hannah paused. She had learned that the signs of the Lord's presence were all around her if only she would listen. No answers came to her immediately, but she felt peace wash over her so she kept walking.

The trail wound through thick stands of trees as it followed the creek that meandered through the valley that separated her family's farm from that of her beau, Abram. Just thinking about him now sent a flush creeping up her neck. The two had been sweethearts since they were children, and she assumed that eventually the two would marry. Lately, though, he had seemed...distant...almost secretive.

No, she was just being silly, she told herself. She brushed off her concerns, and tried to concentrate on listening to an answer to her questions. Once she'd started thinking about Abram, though, she found that she was too distracted to focus.

A branch snapped to her right, and Hannah froze. There weren't any wild animals that she needed to be worried about. Still, she turned toward the sound, watching, and waiting warily. Another branch snapped, and Hannah felt uneasy for a moment.

"Abram!" she exclaimed as her beau stepped out from behind the trees. Her breath caught in her chest, but she was glad to see him.

"Hannah," Abram said, a frown creasing his forehead as he saw her. She returned his frown. Why didn't he seem happy to see her? "What are you doing out here?"

"Just taking a walk," she said, still frowning at him. "I have a lot to think about, to pray about."

"You should be careful," he said, nodding once before he reached toward her. He pulled her into a quick hug before setting her on her path toward home. "I'll come by later."

And with that he disappeared back into the trees.

Part Two:

The next morning Hannah woke up with a headache. Her maemm and daed had sat all of them down the night before to tell them about the most recent cattle thefts. Hannah had to pretend that she didn't know what they were talking about, but every now and then she had glanced at her brothers and sisters, who all seemed genuinely shocked. She couldn't blame them. After the last set of thefts, the local sheriff had seemed to think that he had caught the person who was responsible. This latest theft proved that theory wrong.

"I don't understand," Mary said. Hannah turned toward her sister who was only eleven months younger than her. The two of them often thought alike, but Mary often said what was on her mind, where Hannah kept her mouth shut, content to watch and listen. Now she was curious to hear what her sister had to say. Mary continued, "The sheriff said that he caught the man responsible, so does this mean that someone else is now stealing our cattle or that they didn't get the right person?"

Their daed shook his head slowly, and Hannah couldn't help but notice how weary he looked as he told them all that he simply didn't have any good answers for them.

Now as Hannah slowly sat up in bed, she realized that Abram had never come by last night. She wondered what had kept him, but she couldn't use up her brain space wondering about that. She still hadn't gotten the answer to her prayers that she had been seeking, and now in the bright morning light, she wondered if that was because she had gotten distracted during her prayer time yesterday. Was the lack of an answer a punishment for not being faithful enough? Hannah knew that she needed to get her chores done so she could get outside to go for another prayer walk.

Hurrying to dress, Hannah noticed that Mary had already awoken. Hannah wondered if her sister had the same sense of urgency to figure out how to help their parents out of this situation. "I'll feed the chickens, Maemm," Hannah called as she whirled through the kitchen.

"No need," her maemm said, halting Hannah's progress as she reached out her hand to the back door. "Mary's already done that. If you could start the eggs for breakfast that would be wonderful."

Hannah didn't hesitate to pull out the large, chipped ceramic bowl that they used to stir the eggs in when they made scrambled eggs for breakfast. After she had cracked twelve eggs, Hannah added some heavy cream that had been brought in from their milk cow, Daisy. That was Hannah's not-so-secret secret for making perfect eggs. She added some salt and pepper before taking the whisk, and beating air into them until the yolks looked light and fluffy.

"Do you mind if I go for a walk after my chores are done?" Hannah asked.

"As long as you are back by dinner time," her maemm answered.

Hannah took the cast iron skillet to the stove, and made the eggs while the rest of her siblings drifted into the kitchen, some fresh in from their morning chores. While they sat down to eat, Hannah's mind drifted to Abram's absence once again. She couldn't help but wonder if something had happened to their cattle. The thought made Hannah's stomach tighten with worry. She would have to stop over there after her prayer walk. Her leg jiggled as she felt her impatience rise. When had her family become such slow eaters?

"Daughter, what is wrong with you this morning? You look like a cat dropped in a bucket of water," her daed said.

Blinking at him in surprise, Hannah shook her head as she flushed. "No, I'm fine. I apologize," she said. "I didn't sleep well. I'm just looking forward to getting outside to tend the garden."

Her daed studied her for a long moment before he nodded. "I heard that Abram has been looking to start his own herd of cattle," he remarked.

Hannah's flush deepened at the implication of that statement. She looked at her plate of eggs and sausage. "I don't know about any of that," she told her family before anyone else could say anything.

"I heard that Abram's daed lost four sheep yesterday," Benjamin announced between forkfuls of egg.

At that news, Hannah's head snapped up. That must have been the reason that Abram hadn't come over last night. She should go over to console the family. Up until now, Abram's family had avoided falling victim to the thefts. Their sheep herd was prized in the community, and

Abram's daed had spent his whole life building the herd to be what it was.

It took everything in her to keep her leg still as she finished her breakfast. After everyone had finished eating, Mary offered to help her wash up. When the two of them were alone, Mary asked, "Do you think that Abram is going to propose soon?"

"How should I know?" Hannah asked, feeling the flush rise up her cheeks again. "We haven't really talked about that."

Mary arched an eyebrow. "You've been together for years."

"Oh, fine, we've talked about getting married, and I assume it will happen, but it will have to happen when he's ready," Hannah said. "And if his family has been affected by the thefts, then I don't know when that will be."

Part Three:

Taking a deep breath, Hannah walked up the driveway that led to Abram's house. Her stomach was in knots, and she didn't know how she was going to ask him to help, especially if his own family was now hurting from the rash of thefts. The answer to her prayers had come to her as she had hurried over to Abram's house after she had finished her chores

As she walked she had prayed a quick prayer that she knew wasn't her best one. *Dear Lord,* she prayed, *I know that I'm not praying as deeply as I should, but I need your help. How do I help my family out of this mess? Amen.*

Before she had even had the chance to knock on the front door, it swung open, and Abram's younger sister, Lucy, launched herself at Hannah in a full throttle hug. "Hannah! I haven't seen you in ages," the younger girl cried with delight.

Hannah hugged her back, and couldn't help but chuckle. "Is Abram home?" she asked as Lucy dragged her inside.

"Oh, he's out back helping daed count the sheep. Daed actually thought that four of the sheep had been stolen like all those cattle! Can you believe that?" Lucy exclaimed.

"They weren't?" Hannah asked, confusion slipping through her resolve to ask Abram for help.

"No, they were just lost in the south pasture," Lucy said as she shook her head. "They really caused quite a stir, though. Daed said that your folks lost some more cattle. I'm really sorry about that, Hannah. Do you think they'll ever catch the guy?"

Hannah felt the weight of her family's situation crash down on her, but she did her best to pull a brave smile up on her face. "I sure hope so," she said.

"Sit here and I'll go get the cookies I made this morning," Lucy said, and before Hannah could say anything else, Lucy had disappeared into the kitchen.

Hannah wanted to call after her that really she just wanted to see Abram. The stress of her family's situation was weighing on her so heavily that she needed to share it with someone. She felt God's call before she could put words to it, and in an instant she knew that she needed to share it with the Lord first and foremost.

So while Lucy was still puttering around in the kitchen Hannah bowed her head, and began to pray. *Dear Lord, I'm sorry for my lack of humility. Forgive me for my stupidity. My heart is aching for my parents and for my family. I need your help to bear this cross. I know that you will keep us safe, and guide us through this storm. Amen.*

She finished her prayer just as Lucy came in with a plateful of cookies. A feeling of peace descended on her, and even though she didn't have any more answers than she had started with, she was able to eat a few of the sugar cookies without feeling the need to rush through the visit. Lucy did most of the talking, and Hannah listened with a smile tugging the corners of her mouth.

When they had finished, Hannah stood, and dusted her crumb covered hands on her apron. "I'm just going to pop out back to say hello to Abram. You should stop by our house soon," Hannah told Lucy. "Mary's been making some chocolate chip cookies that you would love"

Slipping through the always warm kitchen, Hannah said hello to Abram's maemm before she stepped out onto the back porch. From where she stood she could see the whole of the farm with the big milking barn and the horse barn, and the small sheds that housed the chickens and goats. Beyond all of that was the large barn that housed the sheep. Green fields spread out in every direction butting up against the woods that separated Abram's family farm from her own family's farm.

She was still looking at the beauty of the farm when she caught sight of Abram and his daed coming out of the barn. They looked like they were deep in conversation so she waited until there seemed to be a lull in their conversation before she waved and called, "Abram!"

Abram turned, and she thought that she saw a frown flit across his handsome features before he waved her toward them. Hannah tried to shake off her moment of unease, before she hurried over. Abram's daed greeted her before he headed back into the house.

"I missed you yesterday," Hannah said.

"Yeah, I'm sorry about that," Abram said. "My daed thought that some of his sheep had been stolen so I had to go out searching for them in the dark. We found them eventually, but it was still a long night."

Something flashed through the edge of Hannah's mind, but she couldn't pin it down. "My daed lost more cattle last night," Hannah said with a sigh.

"I heard about that this morning," Abram said, glancing back at the barn, seeming distracted. "I'm sorry about that."

A bawling cry from the back of the barn drew their attention, and Hannah stepped toward it. Through the dimly lit interior of the barn she could see several calves on the other side. Before she could ask Abram about it, he was already guiding her away.

Still distracted, Hannah blurted, "Abram, you have to help us. How will my family survive all these thefts? We can't afford a new bull."

An uncomfortable look crossed Abram's face, and that discomfort made the thought flit through Hannah's mind again. Something about the way Abram had been so distant lately, and now the way he was shuffling her away from the barn and toward the path home.

"Listen," he said. "I have some things that my daed needs me to attend to, but I promise that I'll stop by later."

And once again, he strode off without another backward glance.

Part Four:

She couldn't believe that she was actually beginning to think that Abram could have anything to do the thefts. Still, as she hurried down the path through the woods, tears blurring her vision, all she could think about were the five new calves in the back stall of the barn. Where had he gotten them? A purchase like that would be big news throughout their community.

Tears burned the backs of her eyes. She had spent so many years assuming that she and Abram would be married and start a family together that she had missed the part where they were growing apart. But had they? Were they? The questions pounded at her temples as she moved faster through the woods.

By the time she got home, she was more confused than ever. Not wanting to let her family see her crying, Hannah made her way to the horse barn where she climbed up into the hay loft. No one would think to look for her there.

The sweet smelling hay surrounded her like a cloud, hiding her away from the rest of the world. The problems that had been swirling around her seemed to drift away for a few moments. When she was a little girl she had come up here after fights with friends or sisters, and when she could spend a few minutes alone with God, she felt better.

God, where are you? She prayed quietly. She didn't want to be a person who lost her faith just because of hardship or strife, but suddenly she felt overwhelmed by the enormity of the situation that she and her family were facing.

Rustling at the foot of the ladder caused Hannah to prop herself up on her elbows. Mary's concerned face popped up over the side of the hayloft floor. Hannah allowed herself to flop back down on to the hay.

"Are you okay?" Mary asked. "I saw you make a beeline over here when you came out of the woods. I thought you might need some company."

Mary climbed into the hay with her, and settled down. The two lay in silence for a long while, and Hannah appreciated her sister's ability to understand her moods. Finally Hannah said, "Do you think that anything will be okay?"

"I'm not sure what exactly you are talking about, but if it's about the cattle thefts, I think it's going to be really hard for maemm and daed to recover. Daed might have to try to find outside work again." Mary paused. "That's not all that you are talking about is it?"

Hannah sighed. "No, it's not. Can I tell you something?"

"Of course," Mary said, propping herself up on her elbow.

"But you can't tell anyone," Hannah said. She took a deep breath. "I think that maybe Abram is involved in the thefts somehow."

"Don't be ridiculous," Mary said. "This is Abram we're talking about."

"He's been so distant lately," Hannah said, barreling on. "And there are at least four new calves in his barn."

Mary got quiet at that news, but she shook her head. "I still think that you aren't seeing the situation clearly. I don't mean to be rude about it, but how can you even think that about Abram. Don't you love him?"

"Of course I do!" Hannah exclaimed, feeling her heart squeeze in her chest.

"Then, I don't understand, how can you suspect him of something so awful?" Mary asked.

Hannah blinked up at the barn's high ceiling. Her sister had a good point. How could she? "I can't explain it," she said. "Even though I love him with all my heart, I guess I've just been looking for an answer so hard that I was willing to see signs everywhere I looked. I was imposing my own will instead of letting God's will be done. I'll have to make a confession before the bishop."

The sisters fell silent again for a long time. "So what are you going to do?" Mary finally asked.

"I don't know," Hannah said. Sitting up, she brushed hay off her dress. "But I'm going to pray about it. And this time, I'm really going to listen with my whole heart."

Part Five:

The darkness pressed in on her, and Hannah pulled her shawl tighter around herself. Hannah knew that she was on a fool's errand, and that she was probably putting herself in harm's way, but she couldn't see any other way. At worst Abram might be involved in the thefts, and at best he had simply been unwilling to help.

She held the flashlight that she had pulled out of her daed's tool chest in the barn, but she was determined not to turn it on until it was absolutely necessary. The moon lent a faint glow to the path around the far pasture, but Hannah was determined to stay near the fence. If she followed the weathered wooden rails, then she knew she wouldn't get lost.

Somewhere in the distance a cow called out, sounding startled. Hannah paused, listening hard for other noises. Hearing nothing, she continued her trek around the pasture fence. When she had thought this plan through she had figured that the best place to watch and wait for the cattle thieves was down by the gate that was closest to the main road. She just hadn't figured out how hard it would be to get over there.

"What do you think you're doing?"

Hannah stifled a scream as she spun around to see Mary carrying a lantern coming up behind her. "Mary! What are you doing here?" Hannah asked in a hushed, exasperated whisper.

"That's exactly what I am asking you," Mary retorted, propping her hand on her hip. The lantern in her other hand bobbed and swung precariously.

"Blow that out," Hannah said, lunging toward her sister. "What if they see it?"

"Who?" Mary asked as she moved the lantern out of her sister's way.

"The cattle thieves," Hannah said. "That's why I'm out here. I want to prove once and for all that Abram isn't involved in this mess, and at the same time find out who is responsible so that we can get our cattle back."

Even in the dim moonlight Hannah could see Mary looking at her in disbelief. "I don't think that's such a good idea," she finally said.

Hannah laughed, and then clapped a hand over her mouth. She looked around quickly. Seeing no one, she turned her attention back to her younger sister. "It's too late for that now," she said. "I need to see this through. I just...I have to know. I hope you can understand that."

"I don't understand," Mary admitted, "but that doesn't affect the fact that I will support you no matter what. I'll come with you. There's strength in numbers after all."

Hannah felt a surge of warmth and love toward her sister. "Thank you," she whispered. "Now the plan is to go around the perimeter of the fence until we get to the gate that leads to the main road. I figure that's the most likely place to see if the cattle thieves come tonight."

As they walked forward Mary asked, "And then what?"

"Honestly, I don't know," Hannah admitted.

"Why do you think they'll come here tonight?" Mary asked.

"I don't know that they'll come here tonight, but I am planning to it here every night until they do come back," Hannah said with more confidence than she felt.

Mary propped her hand on her hip, and sighed. "And then what?" she repeated. "Hannah, if you are going to come up with a harebrained plan, then you have to think it all the way through."

"Actually I'm not sure that I do need to think it all the way through," Hannah said, pressing her lips together to suppress a smile, despite the fact that her sister wouldn't be able to see it anyway. "The definition of harebrained allows me to only think through the first part."

"Hannah, really," Mary said with such exasperation that Hannah couldn't help but giggle. Even in the strange circumstances she found herself in, her sister still made her laugh. "Actions have consequences."

"I know that actions have consequences," Hannah snapped. "But this was all I could think of. Do you have a better suggestion?"

Mary spread out her hands. "I think it's a little late for that, don't you?"

"Well, then you have two choices, you can either stay with me and see what happens, or you can go back home," Hannah said, wrapping her hand around the flashlight before she turned away. I don't have any more choices. I have to find out who is trying to ruin our family, and I need to clear Abram's name."

"Well, obviously I have to come with you," Mary said. "I couldn't live with myself if I went home and then something happened to you."

Hannah nodded, but didn't say anything as she began walking again. Despite the fact that she had been all bluster when suggesting that her sister return to the house, Hannah was secretly glad that her sister was coming with her. There was always safety in numbers...though Hannah wasn't sure that either of them would be safe if they ended up coming face to face with the cattle thieves.

When the two got to the end of the fence, Hannah instinctively dropped down into a crouch. She yanked down her sister, and motioned for Mary to be quiet. Hannah wasn't sure what had caused her to feel like the two of them were threatened, but she knew, she just knew, that there was something out there that made her alert.

A flash of light from the opposite side of the road, near the woods, made Mary gasp beside her, and Hannah gripped her sister's arm. In her mind she was telling herself that they needed to remain quiet, but her body ignored her brain.

Clutching the flashlight in her hand, Hannah let go of her sister, and leapt to her feet. With her heart pounding in her throat, she shouted, "You! Over there! Stop where you are! I know what you are doing, and I'm not going to let you get away with it!"

Part Six:

"Hannah?"

The sound of total disbelief in Abram's voice made her stomach cramp. She should have known that her discovery was too good to be true. For one triumphant moment, Hannah had been sure that she had caught the cattle thieves. Even as her mind had scrambled to figure out what to do next, she had been thrilled to think that she had finally solved her family's problem. Her heart was beating so hard in her chest that she thought it might break right in front of Abram.

"Yes, it's me," Hannah replied, trying—and failing—to keep the tears out of her voice.

"What are you doing out here?" Abram asked, still sounding confused.

"I could ask the same of you," Hannah said, pushing her broken heart aside. She was going to put an end to this once and for all.

Abram took a step toward her, and Hannah instinctively took a step back. She hated that this was how she was acting with the man she loved—-and she did still love him dearly—but all the evidence that she had at her disposal pointed to Abram being the culprit.

"It isn't safe for you to be out here," Abram said, stepping closer.

"Why?" Hannah asked. She needed him to tell her the truth, even if it wasn't something that she wanted to hear.

"If the cattle thieves show up again—" Abram was cut off by the sound of an engine revving in the distance. Swiftly, he grabbed the flashlight out of her hand, clicked it off, and pulled her down below the fence line so that they wouldn't be seen.

Hannah's heart began to pound in her chest, and her temples began to throb as she realized that even though she didn't know exactly what was going on, she had her evidence that Abram wasn't involved. But, then, why was he out here so late at night?

When she asked him that exact question, she could feel him grimace. "I should be asking you the same thing," he muttered. "But I'm out here as part of a community patrol that your daed set up. We've been watching for the cattle thieves at different farms for weeks, but so far we haven't been able to catch them."

Hannah's cheeks flamed with embarrassment and shame. "Abram, I have something to tell you," she said softly.

"What? Are you going to confess that you're one of the cattle thieves?" he asked.

The humor in his voice only made the situation worse. Taking a deep breath, Hannah said, "I thought you might be involved. In the thefts, I mean. I don't know why. Well, maybe I do. I was so worried about my family that I was looking for an answer wherever I could see one. I'm so sorry. When you started to get distant, I didn't know what to think. And I thought the worst. I understand if you are angry with me. And I understand if you never want to see me again."

To her amazement, Abram burst out in laughter that he quickly stifled. "I don't mean to laugh at you," he said with all the seriousness he could muster. "But why didn't you just come to me with your concerns? We could have cleared all this up, and you wouldn't have had to feel the need to come out in the middle of the night to stalk dangerous cattle thieves."

"You're still teasing me," Hannah pointed out, although she was beginning to feel herself relax.

"Maybe just a little," Abram admitted. "But only because you seem so upset."

"Well, I thought that you might be destroying my family's livelihood, so I think that it will take a moment longer before I feel cheerful again," Hannah said. She heard the distress still in her voice, creeping out as she spoke.

"It does hurt that you would think that of me," Abram said after a long moment of silence. "But I can understand that you needed to put the pieces together."

Hannah stepped forward, and reached out to take Abram's hand. "I am sorry that I suspected you," she said. "But I'm sorrier that I didn't come talk to you about my concerns. Well...I did try one day, but you and your daed were busy, and then I saw the calves, and well..."

"You saw the calves?" Abram's voice sounded choked and higher than normal. "You weren't supposed to see the calves."

Another shot of fear went through Hannah's stomach. Could it be that Abram was still somehow involved in the cattle thievery? Could he be lying to her? She thought through the conversation that they had just had, and she decided that she knew Abram. She knew his heart, and she had been praying for answers. She loved him, and she knew that she had been wrong to doubt him. She still had a lot of questions, though, and she knew that she needed to be bold to ask him.

"I saw the calves," she confirmed. "What were they for Abram? How did you find the money to buy four calves? I thought...I thought that you were saving for our future."

Abram sighed, and dropped Hannah's hand so he could run both hands through his hair. In the dim light of the glow from the flashlight, she could see the hair sticking up in all different directions. She thought that he looked as frazzled as she felt.

"They were, are, for our future," Abram said. "The calves, I mean. They are for our future. I took out a loan from my daed to buy them. I'm going to raise them, sell them, and after I pay back my daed, buy some more. I just thought that it would be better to make a small profit before I told you about them, but I can see now that I should have shared my thoughts with you."

"That would have been nice," Hannah agreed. "But I guess I can see why you did that."

A silence descended upon them, but Hannah still had other questions. She still had other thoughts that she needed to share with him, but she knew that now wasn't the time for a long conversation. Suddenly she was aware of the other men from the community patrol milling about on the edge of her vision, along with her daed and Mary. If she hadn't been so intent on getting answers, she would have felt intense embarrassment.

"When were you going to tell me?" Hannah asked, deciding that was the next right question that she wanted an answer to.

Abram shuffled his feet, and said," Right after I proposed to you."

Hannah knew that she had heard him correctly, but she had to ask him anyway. "When were you going to propose to me?"

"I was planning on doing it soon, but I thought it might be better as a surprise," Abram said. "But I suppose this is as good a spot as anywhere."

As his words sank into her brain, Hannah felt her heart beat faster, the sound of blood throbbing in her ears drowning out all the noise around them. He was going to ask her to marry him right now, in this moment. And then she realized that he was actually doing it. She heard him say, "I'd be honored if you'd be my wife."

"Yes," Hannah said as it echoed through her heart. "But wait. Can we really do this here? Now?"

Abram laughed. "Of course we can."

"But we're all out here trying to catch cattle thieves," Hannah groaned. "What if they came around the corner right now? They could be heavily armed. They could hurt all of us."

"We're fine," Abram said. "The thieves seem to have a pattern. None of us think that they'll try anything tonight, and if they did we are more than ready for them. This, right here, the two of us are more important than any of that."

"Then yes," Hannah said feeling her worries break away and elation rise up in her chest like she hadn't in weeks. "I would absolutely love to be your wife."

After the two of them had hugged, Hannah hurried over to her sister and her daed to tell them what had just transpired. While her daed went to talk to Abram and to shake his hand. When their daed had gone, Mary grabbed Hannah with a small squeal, and said, "So I guess he wasn't stealing our cattle, huh?"

Embarrassment raced through Hannah, but she knew that the Lord had given her all the answers she needed, and that she needed to be humble in her mistakes. "Of course not," she said. "I was wrong, but that's all part of being human. God has led us to this point, and He will continue to lead us wherever we need to go."

As she glanced over at Abram and her daed, Hannah was struck by the exact answer to her prayers, her past and her future blending seamlessly together. And she realized that by trusting the Lord, even with the uncertainties of life, she didn't have any reason to fear.

A Little Bit of Amish Faith

Alana Wilson

The streets were just beginning to get dark as Nicholas drove home. He can still hear his boss's, no, ex-boss's words echoing in the back of his mind, *I'm sorry Nicky, but we can't keep you employed if you have to call in every other day with a family emergency. It's just not how business works...* Nicholas felt himself grinding his teeth as he sped down the poorly lit backroad to his house. His headlights flashed across the wet asphalt as his mind wandered. *How am I going to tell my mom? How am I going to get groceries now and her medicine?* His mind ran circles. His headlights flashed across trees as his truck hit a patch of ice and skid. Nicholas turned the wheel hard and tried to correct the vehicle in time.

His headlights flashed across a figure that dove out of the way of his vehicle as it careened towards the ditch. Nicholas finally regained control and swerved hard. His truck skidded to a stop on the shoulder. Nicholas opened the door and slid out of the driver seat; adrenaline rushed through his body. He took shaky steps to the edge of the road. He peered down into the ditch, looking for the dark figure. They lay in the dirty snow. Nicholas slid down the bank to the figure's side. He saw in the pale twilight that it was a girl; she wore a thick dark coat over a plain dark blue dress and a starched white cap on her head. She groaned and sat up slowly.

"Are you okay?" Nicholas felt his heart pounding in his ears and his hands trembled.

"I, I think so." She replied quietly. He helped her to her feet and she groaned, leaning into him.

"I think I twisted my ankle," she said with a grimace.

"I'm so sorry. Let me take you to a doctor." Nicholas started to almost drag her up the ditch.

"Oh, no. That won't be necessary. I'm fine, really." She said shyly.

"Please let me take you to a doctor, or at least somewhere we can look at your ankle in the light." He looked at her pleadingly. He could almost see her debating it internally.

"I guess it wouldn't hurt to get it looked at, just in case it is serious," she said quietly. He sighed in relief. They scrambled up the bank to Nicholas's truck. He helped her into the passenger seat and scrambled around to his side.

"I'm so sorry, again. I didn't see you and the road was slick... I'm just so sorry." He trailed off as he looked at her face; she had a few minor scratches and scrapes.

"I forgive you. Everything happens for a reason; that is God's plan." She glanced out the window distantly.

"What are you even doing out here?" He tried to keep one eye on her and one eye on the road.

She was pretty, even in the dim light. Nicholas could see wisps of dark brown hair peeking out from under her cap and her dark green eyes were glassy. A light blush colored her cheeks. Nicolas caught a glimpse of his own nervous brown eyes in the mirror.

"I was walking back from the bakery in town. My uncle and aunt own it, and I work there whenever they need a hand. With the holidays around the corner, they're starting to get backed up with orders."

"You think they need any other help?" He chuckled nervously. She didn't respond. He drove the truck in silence. She held her hands clasped tightly in her lap.

"What's your name?" He finally said, breaking the tense silence.

"Naomi." She muttered.

"I'm Nicholas." He smiled at her.

He parked the truck outside the clinic in town. He helped Naomi out of the truck and inside. Doctor Schaffer sat at the front desk, working on paperwork; she was a middle aged woman, with streaks of gray coloring her ashy blonde hair and wrinkle just starting to appear at the corners of her eyes and mouth.

"Nicholas? Naomi? What are you two doing here so late at night? And together?" She said, and walked around the counter. Nicholas couldn't help but stare between the doctor and Naomi.

"Good evening, doctor. Nicholas here found me after I took a spill down the ditch outside town. I think I twisted my ankle." Naomi smiled sweetly up at the doctor. The doctor tutted and shook her head.

"Well, let's take you back and have a look at that ankle. Nicholas, would you mind giving me a hand here," Doctor Shaffer said, helping Naomi to her feet. Nicholas helped Naomi hobble to the exam room down the hall and onto the table.

"Well, I'll be on my way then. Will you be all right getting home, miss?" Nicholas edged towards the doorway.

"Nicolas, if you could take a seat in the waiting room, actually. I'll check on Naomi, and if it's too serious for my taste, I want you to drive her home so she doesn't overstrain herself." Doctor Shaffer smiled at Nicholas and ushered him out of the room. Nicolas wandered back to waiting room and slumped into a chair. He felt the weight of the day on his shoulders. *How could I be so stupid? I lose my job, I almost kill someone... I need to get my act together and fast,* he thought to himself. He rubbed his eyes and tried to shake the weariness.

Naomi hobbled down the hall on a crutch, back to the waiting Nicholas. He smiled shyly at her. Doctor Shaffer shuffled down the hall behind her.

"Okay, Naomi has a severe sprain and needs to stay off her ankle for a few weeks," Doctor Shaffer said, looking between the two.

"Thanks, Doc." Nicholas held open the door as Naomi hobbled outside. Nicholas helped her back into the truck. They drove down the road in silence.

"I'm sorry. Again."

"It all happened for a reason." Naomi looked out the passenger window thoughtfully.

Farms passed by as Nicholas drove down the back roads that led to the Amish community. He slowed down as the roads turned from asphalt to gravel. He stopped the truck at the gate of their community.

His headlights couldn't pierce the darkness that stretched further down the road.

"Do you need any help?" He turned to her. She looked at him, almost glared.

"No. I'll be just fine. I think you've done enough," she snarled at him and slammed the door open. She slid out of the truck and started to hobble down the dirt road. Nicholas followed her.

"Okay, I understand if you're upset. I messed up big time tonight, and you're nothing more than an innocent bystander. Please, let me try to make this right." He almost reached for her hand. Almost.

"No, this is far enough. I will be shunned by my community if they see me with you, especially in your vehicle. I can make it from here. Thank you for everything, but I hope we do not meet again in the future." She brushed an angry tear from her cheek and turned away from him.

"Let me walk with you, then. It's too dark and cold to be alone." She sighed heavily.

"Fine. But after tonight, I wish to never speak to you again," she glared at him and continued on her way.

"That's fair." Nicholas shrugged.

They walked down the dark country road in utter silence. Nicholas kept stealing glances at Naomi, trying to read her face. It occurred to him at that moment, this was the first time he had really forgotten about himself. He thought about her instead. *Is she married yet? I know the Amish girls get married young...* His thoughts wandered to who she was, what her life was like. He didn't think any more about his mother and brother waiting for him at home, or the heaviness in his heart from his father's recent passing, or the weariness in his joints from working all hours of the day.

She stopped at a tall white farm house. An old woman sat on the porch, reading by the light of a lantern. Nicholas stood at the bottom of the stairs as Naomi shuffled onto the porch. The old woman mumbled something at her. Naomi sighed and turned back to Nicholas. The old woman nodded and stood creakily.

"Nicholas, thank you for your assistance," she said quietly.

He opened his mouth to say something but she ducked inside before the words came out. Nicholas raised his hand in an awkward wave and walked back down the road. The darkness enveloped him, but for the first time in a long time, he felt clear headed. He walked in the chilly autumn night.

Nicholas sat in his truck outside his little two-story house. All the lights were off. The clock on the radio read 11:53. He trudged inside wearily. In the living room, his mother was asleep on the couch. His old lab, Gunner, greeted him at the front door with a small huff. Nicholas woke his mother up with a gentle shake.

"Mom, I'm home. Let's get to bed." He picked her up gently. She seemed to get smaller every day. He carried her down the hall and set her gently in bed. He pulled off her slippers and her fleece robe. She snuggled under the blankets with a soft sigh. He shut her door quietly behind him. Upstairs, he checked on his little brother Kevin. The fifteen-year-old boy lay deep asleep. Nicholas pulled his quilt back on him and walked down the hall to his own room. Nicholas collapsed into his bed, his shoes still on.

Nicholas woke early the next morning. His alarm blared loudly next to him. His crawled out of bed. Nicholas crept down the hall. The sun hadn't risen yet, and neither had anyone else in the house. He drove to town, trying to rub sleep from his eyes. He parked outside the diner in town and trudged inside.

He sat at the counter and drank a cup of black coffee. His phone screen glared back at him, reflecting the harsh facts of his life. *Bank account: $92.63. Mortgage due next Tuesday. Electricity bill due tomorrow.* He couldn't help but sigh heavily into his coffee. He still needed to pick up groceries and his mother's medication. As the sun finally peaked its head fully above the horizon, Nicholas walked down

Main Street. His eyes scanned the buildings looking for any 'help wanted' signs, but there were none to be seen.

But as he walked on, he did see something interesting; Naomi walking on her crutches down the other side street. Her face was red from exertion. He crossed the street at a jog and came to a stop in front of her.

"Morning," he croaked shyly.

"Hello," she growled and tried to move around him.

"Wait." He almost reached for. She stopped to listen, but didn't turn to look at him.

"I'm sorry, for last night. Do you need any help? The bakery is still a bit down the road and I'm sure it's taken you all morning to get to this point."

"And?" She snarled again.

"Let me give you a ride. Please. I want to make up for my actions," he pleaded. She was silent for a moment and then sighed.

"I guess I'm no use to my aunt if I show up at the end of the day."

"Great. Just wait here, I'll get my truck." Nicholas raced off to get his truck and pulled up next to Naomi.

They drove down the road quietly. The radio played a quiet news report, the only sound in the small cab of the truck. The bakery was just outside of town, a tourist trap. The building was squat, white-washed and impeccably clean. The parking lot was just a gravel lot. It smelled like fresh-baked bread and cinnamon rolls. He parked and helped her out of the truck.

"Well, I don't think I need any further assistance. Thank you, Nicholas." She shuffled into the bakery. Nicholas watched her go, feeling some small tug towards her. He let his feet carry his to the door and then inside. Naomi hobbled to the back on her crutches. A middle-aged woman, dressed in the same clothes as Naomi came out.

"Good morning, how can I help you?" She smiled politely at Nicholas.

"Oh, I was wondering if I could help you actually. I'm an acquaintance of Naomi's and I know she has a pretty bad sprain, so I was hoping I could help out until she's feeling better." He felt his cheeks burn. The woman studied him for a minute. She raised a finger to him and the disappeared into the back. He could hear the hushed voices as Naomi and the woman talked. The woman came back and looked Nicholas up and down.

"If you'd like to help, you are to be here from dawn to dusk. What is your work ethic like?"

"I'm willing to do anything. I can lift things and I'm good with tools and I can be here early or late or whatever you need." His heart raced. Naomi glared at him from the doorway.

"Alright then. You'll be paid every week, in cash of course. How does $300 a week sound? And this will be temporary, just until Naomi is back on her feet." The woman laughed now. Nicholas smiled.

"This is great. I can start right now. If you need me to." He felt giddy now.

"Ay, get back there and start moving those flour sacks from the back door to the pantry." He slid past the woman and almost tripped over Naomi's crutch.

Nicholas was satisfied in this new work. It was labor-intensive, which he didn't mind. But what he liked the most was picking up Naomi in the mornings. She had gotten permission from her community for Nicholas to pick her up at the gates and to drive her to work. They would talk sometimes early in the morning, about their favorite books, the weather, their families. He learned so much about her; she lived with her aunt and uncle, who owned the bakery she worked at, and her grandmother lived with them. She shared a room with her six cousins; four boys and two girls. She learned that he lived with his mother and younger brother. He had worked many job since dropping out of high school to take care of sick mother. He had played a game called lacrosse in school and he tried to explain the game to her on multiple occasions.

When they worked together, Nicholas couldn't help but look at Naomi from time to time. Her aunt had set up a stool at the front counter so she wouldn't have to stand all day. He would sometimes stare, and then catch himself and get back to work. He would chastise himself every time. But he couldn't help but notice how pretty she would look, like when she had smidges of flour smeared on her face or the smile she would use when her uncle told a joke while they sat in the kitchen baking loaf after loaf of bread. But she looked the nicest when they sat in his truck after work, when the sun came in the passenger window just right and caught a few stray hairs that had slipped out from under her cap during the day and made her cheeks look rosy and full. One day, after Nicholas had worked been driving her for a few weeks, Naomi looked at him curiously.

"I understand that you live with your mother and brother, but would you mind if I asked what happened to your father?"

"He didn't run off if that's what you're asking," Nicholas chuckled," He was, uh, killed a few months ago in a drunk driving accident. It's been rough on my mom and Kevin, but it's been getting better."

"I'm sorry to hear that. My parents passed when I was quite young. Also from an auto accident." She looked down at her hands soberly.

"That sucks. I'm sorry that happened to you. Doesn't God just have a sick sense of humor?" Nicholas wanted to punch himself in the face for opening his stupid mouth.

"God doesn't have a sense of humor. Everything He plans, it is for a reason." She replied calmly.

"Oh really? So God killed my dad and made my mother sick for some important reason," Nicholas snarled at her.

"Yes. What is your mother sick with?" She studied Nicholas's face.

"Cancer. It's terminal."

"I'm sorry. But did you think ever think God gives His hardest battles to His most worthy children?" She smiled at him.

"Why?" Nicholas stared straight ahead at the road.

"Because there will always be evil in the world and God must make sure He has soldiers to fight that evil, on earth and from heaven," she said, getting a powerful air behind her voice. Something intense, passionate.

"So, my mom and dad are soldiers for God?" Nicholas scoffed lightly.

"Most likely. If not, then they have a good place in heaven for them, something peaceful and rewarding." She smiled peacefully, as if thinking about what Heaven looks like.

"That's, that's actually really nice to think about. Thank you, Naomi." He noticed from the corner of his eye the small blush creeping up her neck.

Weeks passed and autumn turned into winter. Nicholas became a fixture at the bakery at the edge of town; something was always needing to be fixed and Naomi's cousins were a bit too young to be working there yet. He fixed ceiling tiles and the siding outside. He helped Naomi's uncle repair the window panes and learned how to make everything from a loaf of bread to the biggest wedding cake with pristine white frosting. He discovered he had a knack for frosting cupcakes and kneading dough. He continued to drive Naomi to the bakery and couldn't wait to see her every morning.

"Nicholas, I got you a present," she said one day, sliding a brown paper package across the seat to Nicholas as he picked her up one morning. He raised an eyebrow and opened the present. Inside, a long navy scarf sat folded neatly. He pulled it on and almost blushed; it smelled like Naomi.

"Thank you, this is wonderful Naomi." The thick scarf was warm and soft on his neck.

"Oh, I just thought you could use something warm, since it's cold out and you don't really wear anything besides that jacket," she trailed off as her red nose was matched with a red blush. He reached over and took her hand, looking her in the eye.

"Seriously, thank you, Naomi." She blushed harder and looked away. Nicholas still caught the little smile that stayed on her face for the rest of the day.

Nicholas looked through the window at the jewelry sitting on the velvet display. Everything was going good; the bills were all paid, he had presents for his mother and brother for Christmas. But something was missing. Silver watches and gold chains sat on the black cloth, glittering at him. *I can't afford any of these thing... She probably wouldn't even like it...* He had never seen Naomi wear anything other than her plain dresses and stark white cap. She wore thick gloves and a heavy coat now that it was winter, but she didn't wear makeup or jewelry. He wracked his brain trying to think of something she would actually like.

He walked down the street. It was Sunday night, the only day he got off from the bakery. They were going to close a few days before Christmas and a few days after to celebrate with their community, so Nicholas wanted to get something for Naomi before the holiday. His thoughts wandered as the snow began to fall in thick flakes. He wasn't paying attention and bumped into a girl walking the opposite direction; he knocked the bags from her hands.

"Oh, jeez. I'm so sorry. I didn't mean to." He started to pick up her bags.

"You said that when we first met." She said. Nicholas looked up at her and froze. Naomi stood there, wearing her hair down in soft curls and a cute sweater dress. She wore some makeup, just enough to highlight but not overpower.

"Naomi," he muttered.

"Surprise," she said softly.

"What are you doing here? Don't you need to," he trailed off as he took her in completely.

"I just needed to come into town, and it feels better to look like an English, to blend in better. I saw you from across the street and thought I might surprise you." She smiled and took her bags from him.

"This is a surprise. I was just doing some shopping myself." He blushed slightly.

"Well, then would you mind escorting me home. I like to walk on nights like this when the air is crisp and you can see the stars so clearly." She took his arm and they walked down the street.

They walked quietly for a long time. She grasped his hand firmly; her cold fingers felt so tiny in his. He held her bags in his other hand, like a gentleman. Their breaths billowed in tiny clouds. Cars didn't pass by them in the quiet night. The only sound was their feet crunching through the snow.

"So what did you need to buy," he joked.

"Just a few things from the hardware store. My uncle ran out of nails and he wants to finish up some presents for my cousins so I ran out to get some."

"You're so sweet," he chuckled and squeezed her hand gently.

"So what were you doing in town so late," she teased back.

"Just looking for a present," he shrugged. "For my mom," he added quickly.

"That's very sweet of you, Nicholas. So what were you thinking of getting her?"

"Oh, I can't decide. I wanted to get something nice and fancy for her, but also something practical like a sweater. She does like sweaters. Or a new pair of slippers, ones with thick lining." He had already bought her a thick sweater and a pair of slippers that looked like cats, because she liked silly things like that.

"How about some thick socks?" Nicholas laughed hard at her. "Oh, I know, socks! How exciting! But she's sick, so some thick socks would be nice in case her toes are cold," she chuckled softly.

"That's a really good idea, actually. Thank you." He wanted to kiss her. But he didn't. They were friends, co-workers. He didn't want to impose on her beliefs either. He knew that the Amish were conservative and he didn't want to make her uncomfortable. They stopped outside the gates.

"I'll see you tomorrow." She looked up at him, and he swore she batted her eyelashes at him.

"Yeah. Tomorrow. Good night, Naomi." He smiled back as her fingers slipped from his and she took her bag back.

"Good night, Nicholas." She waved at him and walked down the lane.

Nicholas woke early the next morning. His present for Naomi sat on his desk. He grabbed his jacket and crept down the hall, the present tucked under his arm. He snuck to his mother's door and peaked in. She lay there, sleeping peacefully, a small smile on her face. He crossed the room to wake her up. He shook her arm gently. She was cold. He crossed the room and left. On the front porch, he pulled out his phone.

"Hello? Hi, yes, I need an ambulance. I think my mom is dead," he said blankly.

Nicholas sat on the front porch with Kevin. The flashing lights were blindingly bright. An officer squeezed Nicholas's shoulder and gave him a pitiful look. Kevin looked blankly ahead with red rimmed eyes. The paramedic walked down the stairs and stood in front of the boys. She smiled weakly at them.

"I'm sorry boys. Your mom was a good lady. I hear she was a great teacher. She passed in her sleep, so it was painless. She's in a better place now." Nicholas wanted to believe her but he just felt so angry.

After everyone left, it was deathly quiet. Nicholas called into the high school so Kevin wouldn't have to go in. Kevin sat on the couch, wrapped in their mother's favorite blanket. Nicholas didn't know what to say to him. He didn't have any words. *What kind of God orphans a boy?* Nicholas walked down the road aimlessly.

He found himself en route to the bakery and couldn't stop himself. *They would want to know why he was late.* He walked into the warm bakery and saw Naomi's aunt at the counter.

"Nicholas? Are you all right?" She walked around the counter nervously.

"Yeah, I'm fine. My mom died last night," he croaked.

"Oh Nicholas." She hugged him gently. Tears welled in his eyes. Naomi came from the back at that moment.

"Nicholas?" She wiped her hands on rag. He sniffled and left quickly. Outside, in the cold air, tears burned down his face. He heard the down shut behind him and someone grab his hand. He sniffled and wiped the tears roughly from his face.

"Nicholas? I thought you were hurt when you didn't show up this morning." Naomi sounded worried.

"I'm okay. My mom died last night. "He shivered from the cold. He turned to look at her.

"I'm so sorry, Nicholas," she said softly. He took her hands gently.

"Why? Why did she have to die?" He sobbed. Naomi hugged him tightly.

"It's God's will. She's in a better place." She muttered against his coat.

"But why? It's cruel! My brother is orphaned now! We're all alone now. Why would God do that to us?" He cried into her shoulder. She was much shorter than him, but he still held her tightly.

"I don't know, Nicholas. I'm sorry, but I don't have all the answers. Maybe He didn't want her to suffer any longer. And your brother has you. You have each other. You can always build a bigger family." She shushed him and rubbed his back soothingly.

"I don't know what to do any more, Naomi." He rubbed away the tears again.

"Just make it through today. Then make it through tomorrow. And that you aren't alone in this. You have people who will help you." She smiled sweetly up at him. He managed a weak smile back.

"Thank you." He said softly.

"Nicholas, I'm going to go back inside now. It's freezing out here!" She giggled and led him back inside the bakery.

Nicholas sat in the bakery that day, just watching. Naomi's aunt wouldn't let him work, so instead she made him drink hot tea and taste-test pastries. He felt empty inside. But he felt better knowing that Naomi was his friend, at least. She kept glancing at him throughout the day; when she caught his she offered only a smile.

"Nicholas, would you like to walk home with me?" Naomi pulled on her coat tightly as the sun dipped below the horizon.

"Oh, sure." He followed her out the door quietly.

The streets of the town were lit with bright Christmas lights. Nicholas felt tired. He hadn't felt this tired since he had first met Naomi. She took his hand as they walked. He shoved his hand in his other pocket, and felt her present, long forgotten from this morning. He blushed, thinking about how much he had wanted to give it to her in his truck this morning.

"Naomi, I know this is a bad time, but I got you a present. I know I'm not going to see you for like a week, so I wanted to get you something before the holiday. I was going to give it to you this morning but you know..." he trailed off. He took the present out and handed it to Naomi. She smiled up at him.

"Thank you, Nicholas. I know this must be hard." She ripped off the bright red wrapping paper and shoved it in her pocket. She opened the box carefully. Inside, nestled in white tissue paper was a book. It was an old Nancy Drew book of his mother's. He had asked her last night when he got home if he could give it to Naomi.

"I know you said you hadn't read anything good in a long time and my mom had this one lying around. I figured you might like something to read over the holiday and just enjoy." He blushed fiercely under the streetlights.

"Oh, Nicholas. That's so thoughtful. Thank you." She said and kissed his cheek gently. She stowed the book in her own pocket and they walked on. Her fingers laced through his. He felt his heart beating against his rib cage. At the edge of the Amish community, Naomi looked up at him. The night was quiet, peaceful.

"Nicholas, what are we doing," she whispered.

"I don't know. But it's working, isn't it?" He looked deep into her eyes.

"Is it? To be friends is one thing, but to be something more."

"Naomi, let's talk about this later, okay? Let's just be with our families now," he said back tensely.

"You're right. I'm sorry. Go and be with your brother. If you need anything, let me know. Please." She squeezed his hand and turned away from him.

"Thank you, Naomi. For everything," he called to her as she walked down the lane. She looked back over her shoulder and smiled sweetly at him.

At home, Nicholas found his brother asleep on the couch. He slumped against the doorway and rubbed his face. Christmas was just around the corner and it was going to be lonely. Their mother had been the one who set up the Christmas tree and always made them a big breakfast on Christmas morning. He couldn't imagine how empty the couch was going to look on Christmas morning, without their mother sitting there. He woke Kevin up and ushered him to bed. Nicholas collapsed into his own bed, wishing someone were there to hold him. Someone small, with wavy chocolate brown and deep green eyes.

Christmas morning was bleak. Kevin sat glaring at the stack of presents that were for their mother. Nicholas couldn't bear to open the present from his mother. Kevin locked himself in his room. Nicholas opened his mother's presents and cried. Kevin had gotten her a new travel book, for Mongolia. Nicholas stared blankly at the cozy slippers he had bought. Nicholas sat on the porch and read that travel book. He wished he was far away too. He wished he was happy again, wished his brother could be happy again. He wished Naomi was by his side. He wished he had her faith and grace. He looked up as Kevin sat down next to him.

"Hey, Nick."

"How you holding up, buddy?" He closed the book absentmindedly.

"I'm..." He shrugged.

"I'm sorry we can't have a big Christmas dinner or something. Something to make it all..." Nicholas couldn't find the words.

"It's fine. I understand, dude." They sat in silence for a while. The sun began to dip and the snow began falling. Kevin finally stood and went inside. Nicholas sighed. He stood to go inside when he heard someone coming up the gravel driveway. Naomi stood at the bottom of his stairs, holding a basket. She wore her English sweater dress and leggings. A knit hat kept her wavy hair in check.

"Merry Christmas, Nicholas." She said softly.

"Merry Christmas, Naomi. What are you doing here?" Nicholas helped her up the stairs.

"Helping the less fortunate," she teased," Are you going to invite me in? I've got a big dinner that I need to get started."

"Of course, come in." Nicholas was dazed. He took her coat and led her into the kitchen. She smiled sweetly at him as she started cooking. Kevin glanced at him from the stairs.

"You want to come down and meet Naomi? She knows I can't cook and came to make sure you didn't die of starvation," he joked. Kevin shrugged and shuffled down the stairs. Nicholas led him into the kitchen.

"Naomi? Sorry to interrupt, but this is my brother, Kevin. Kevin, this is my friend, Naomi." Naomi smiled and offered her hand. Kevin shook it weakly. Kevin turned to Nicholas.

"She's pretty," he remarked and trudged into living room.

"He seems to be doing okay." She turned back to the cutting board.

"Yeah. He's just jealous he can't snag a nice girl like you," he flirted and then blushed heavily. Naomi blushed slightly too.

"So, how have you been?" She didn't look up from the vegetables she was cutting.

"It's been rough. It's nice to see you, though. I've kind of missed seeing you every day." He pulled a soda out of the fridge and hopped up onto the counter next to her.

"I've missed talking to you, too, Nicholas. It's been quiet. Food will be done in about forty-five minutes." She smiled at him, and Nicholas swore his heart skipped a beat. She looked so natural in his kitchen.

"I finished that book you gave me. And the note inside was sweet." She glanced at him.

"Note?" He raised an eyebrow.

"From your mother? She just said that she was glad I was your friend and that she couldn't be more thankful that somebody had gotten you out of your shell."

"Oh, I didn't know she wrote that. That's so like her." He muttered. He couldn't help but smile at the thought of his mother always looking out for him.

"She must've been quite a woman to have raised you and your brother."

"She was. I miss her." He sipped his soda pensively. Naomi placed her hand on his knee gently. He grasped it and gave her fingers a gentle squeeze.

"Why don't you set the table? It'll only take a few more moments." She smiled gently at him.

They sat around the dinner table. The silence was almost palpable. Kevin poked at the carrots and potatoes on his plate. Nicholas kept stealing glances at Naomi. Naomi didn't take her eyes off her plate either. Nicholas cleared his throat loudly.

"Kevin, what do you think?" Nicholas fixed his younger brother with a hard stare.

"It's good. Thank you, Naomi." He mumbled into his roast potatoes. Nicholas kicked him under the table.

"So, what are you learning in school, Kevin? I didn't get to go to high school," Naomi asked.

"Evolution." Kevin snarled. He stood and left the table.

"Kevin!" Nicholas stood and shouted at him.

"It's okay, Nicholas. He's just feeling hurt. Let him be, he'll come around." Naomi squeezed his hand. Nicholas sat slowly and looked at her. His heart sped up as she battered her lashes slowly at him.

"What are you saying, Naomi?" He felt her small hand in his; it felt like it was two halves made whole.

"Well, if you'll have me, I'd like to stay." She stared at his hands.

"On one condition," he whispered.

"Yes?" She looked deep into his eyes. He could stare at her eyes for forever.

"Kiss me. Please." She smiled and leaned forward slightly. He closed the gap between them and pressed his lips against hers. Time seemed to stop in that second; he was aware of only her in the room. He kept his hands firmly on the table, afraid of startling her like a deer. She leaned back slowly.

"I should go talk to Kevin," Nicholas breathed. His heart still pounded against his chest.

"I'll be right here," she giggled. And unspoken, *I'll be waiting*, hung between them.

Nicholas climbed the stairs and almost ran down the hall to Kevin's room. He knocked loudly. No response. He cracked the door to find Kevin sitting on his bed. Kevin didn't look at him.

"Hey buddy."

"So, your girlfriend is going to be my new mom?" Kevin said blankly. Nicholas sat on the edge of Kevin's bed and sighed.

"No, not at all. She's just here because, I guess, she loves me. She knows what it's like to lose her parents. She's not going to be your new mom or anything more than my girlfriend. But she's going to have a rough time adjusting to this role."

"What?" Kevin looked at Nicholas like Nicholas had grown a second head.

"She's Amish. She's not quite up to date with all the relationship standards of us regular people," he chuckled.

"So?"

"So just come downstairs and give her a chance. Eat something besides a pop tart or ramen. I mean, she did cook us actual food."

"Okay, but just dinner. I'm not sticking around for dessert." Kevin trudged to the door and down the stairs.

As they sat around the table again, Nicholas felt a weight fall off his shoulders, a weight he forgot he was carrying. Nicholas saw his future at that dinner table, and he liked what he saw. He was at peace, at last.

AMISH GUILT

MAYA MILLER

Her mother had always told Rachel, "Darling, divorce is for the weak that do not honor the decisions of our maker," whenever they heard community news or gossip about a broken marriage or divorce. It was just not something that her mother believed should be done – under any circumstances.

And Rachel lived to please others. It was just the way that God had made *her*. She did not want to let her mother down. She did not want to let her community down. She did not believe for a minute that women that chose divorce were weak or sinful, but she feared the pain of being judged as weak. She feared the disappointment that she would incite in her family, especially her mother, if that would ever be something that she would need to consider.

So that was why when her oldest friend in the world, Samuel, encouraged her to sneak away in the night and start a new life, she stubbornly refused. That was why, each and every time she felt the same sickening, sharp, agonizing blows reverberate through her entire physical being, she simply clenched her teeth and prayed for it to be over. And that was why she learned to keep her posture demure even through the pain; her dress and hair completely neat, perfect ad covering her skin; and her flinching at gentle contact by others to a minimum. Others saw a flawless, happy young bride on the verge of entering motherhood with an attentive ad protective husband. Younger girls envied her ability to always carry and dress herself just so, even when they should not have allowed themselves to envy. But what the community did not know, and what they could not see, was that the perfection and poise that she demonstrated to the world was merely the only lifeline she had in an otherwise tumultuous and hopeless reality.

Market day was always Rachel's most and least favorite day. It was her most favorite because she loved having an excuse to leave the house and go out into the community unaccompanied by Walter, or her parents. It was perfectly acceptable in their society for her to do so anytime that she wanted, but her husband did not allow it, with the exception of market day. She was allowed a "stipend," Walter called it, to purchase only necessities for their home and health. "Anything beyond that, you will ask me, and I will give you my answer as to whether I think you need and deserve an item," he had announced on the day after their wedding. He had given her quite a number of instructions that day, in fact. She could not leave the house alone without him or his or her parents; she could not speak with other men within ten years of their age unless he was with her; she was to keep the house clean; she was to only prepare certain meals that he would decree; she was to keep herself presentable; and she was not to argue with him. He continued on from there, with further instructions, and then ended with a level stare into her eyes, stating "and I will punish your insubordination in any way that I see fit. You have been provided by God for me to have dominion over, and I will use that power for whatever I see fit." She had stood on in appalled silence, disguised as obedience, devastated by the fact that she was now tied for her entire life to a cruel, monstrous man.

For the first four months of their marriage, Rachel did her very best to follow the rules and demands of her husband. Inside her head she leveled him with insults and made refusals, stating things like "I am a person and deserve the right to have a rest or enjoy my days" inside her head. But she never uttered such things aloud. In fact, she was productive, obedient and attractive. She lived-up to all the standards in place in the community and more. Her skills were noticed and adopted by others. Her general appearance made those around her smile. Community members assumed that she stayed so much in the house to simply show her husband how much she loved him through her work. He had his way with her ever night, and she was dreading the day that she would realize that she was with child. And through it all, she begged people with her eyes to help her. Sadly no one saw or heard the agony that she was living in.

And then one day it started. She had not seen it coming. She thought that he had already done his worst, denying food or money if she made a mistake. But once the back of Walter's hand made contact with her soft, white cheek, she saw that there was so much more suffering in store for her.

That first backhand slap across the face actually turned out to be a rare even, however. Usually he would save the hits and grips that caused bruises for the parts of her body that would be hidden under the generous clothing that the women of the community wore. It made it easier for him, in his depravity, because the only parts of her body that he really need worry about were her face and upper neck and her hands. Other than there, he had given himself free license over her body, physically and sexually.

Her oldest friend, Samuel, suspected that something was wrong, but she would never confirm it, and warned him to keep quiet about ungrounded suspicions. That particular market day, she was at his family's table at the market, picking out the kinds of vegetables that she by now knew her husband would want. She saw a beautiful squash there that made her mouth water, and placed it in her basket on the ground next to her. But after she thought about it, she realized that purchasing it would mean angering Walter who hated squash. She turned to fetch it from her basket and caught her breath as a shooting pain lanced through her back from the previous night's injuries.

"Rach, what's wrong with your back?" he said as she straightened, more stiffly than she would have liked.

"Oh, nothing. I'm fine," she said as cheerily as she could muster. "I just twisted at a funny angle when I bent down."

Samuel simply stared at her long enough that it became uncomfortable in its obviousness, and Rachel became nervous because she knew from past experience that Walter had spies that would tell him if she was spending too long speaking with any man in particular. He had a huge dislike for Samuel because of their close friendship and had done everything that he could, short of forbidding her to speak to him, to stop that friendship. Samuel was from a well-connected community family, and Walter never picked on the strong, only the weak. The irony of this fact was never lost on Rachel, who had grown-up with that idea that women who left bad marriages were weak – and those that stayed were strong. That should have meant that Walter would not dare pick on her in all of her strength, but obviously there was a disconnect somewhere. Maybe she did not yet know what true strength was, or maybe he was not smart enough to.

"You can't lie to me, Rach. You've never been able to."

She kept that fake public smile plastered to her face and feigned confusion. "I'm not lying, Sammy. I don't have anything to lie about."

"Remember when you stole my jacks on our first day of school?" He retorted with the smallest of half grins.

That brought a genuine smile to her face. "I didn't steal them. You gave them to me," she said in the rehearsed way she always did to keep their old joke going.

"Okay, now that we've established that I won't put up with any lies, can you please tell me what is wrong with your back? Did he do it again?" There was fire in Samuel's eyes now. He had always hated Walter and absolutely loathed him now that he knew that he was rough with Rachel. The reality was that he would likely find a way to kill Walter if he really knew what he did to her, but she had never shared the extent of the behavior. She did not want her friend to be arrested for murder. But Walter dying, that would actually be pretty great.

She felt her cheeks get hot under her best friend's scrutiny. "Sammy, please," she whispered, not really knowing what she was asking him for. She took a step closer and lowered her voice to a quiet whisper. "I don't know how to stop it." The tears that burned the back of her eyes would betray her to anyone watching this conversation, but she was dangerously close to the point where she could no longer blink them back.

Samuel leaned in further – not enough to make the conversation look intimate, but enough so that a passerby at the market would not hear what he was about to say. His eyes softened. "Just leave him. Ask the community for help. Ask *me* for help, Rachel."

"You know I can't just leave him. You know why I can't seek out a divorce."

"Rach, your reasons for not being able to leave him seem pretty weak in the face of the pain that he is causing you. You need to find a way to walk away. I need you to find a way to let yourself get out. Find peace with divorce. Find it in yourself to change your heart about this. I will protect you. I need my best friend alive and kicking, or what have I got? You can use your new heart to make a new start. I can help you."

"It's just not that easy, Sammy. I can't let everyone down. I can't be that person." Her shoulders sagged under the renewed understanding of the situation that she was in. No matter what happened, she would be letting down someone she loved. Her best friend hoped against hope that she would leave, and the rest of the community put faith in what an amazing existence she led and would not understand her walking away.

Samuel straightened up and the anger that was there before flashed anew. "That's not enough of a reason anymore, Rachel. He's hurting you. I know he is, even though you won't show me the bruises he leaves hidden like you on a coward."

"What are you two talking about so privately over here?" The jovial voice of Samuel's father boomed loudly in Rachel's ears and across the market.

Instinctively both she and Samuel took a step back and straightened. "Hi Pa, did you bring the rest of the squash and tomatoes?"

And just like that the conversation was over, at least in that moment. "Well, Sammy, thank you for the beautiful vegetables and I will see you next week." She plastered on her public smile and gave a wave as she turned away, purposefully not looking at his face as she left. To everyone around her it would it would never seem as if Samuel had not just been asking her to make the most difficult decision she had ever had to face. And that is what she needed it to look like until she could figure out what to do.

She always took her time walking home from the market on these days, no matter the weather. Today was a particularly lovely day and she took advantage. She felt like a prisoner that was let out once a week, and she took full advantage of the freedom. She was cognizant of the fact that too much sun could burn her skin, however, and she did not linger too long, as she knew that Walter wanted her skin "white and milky, as a woman should be."

She hated that she was married to a person that would think such a thing. She hated that she was stuck with a husband that was not really a man. And that was just the truth. A real man would not treat a woman the way that her husband did. And Samuel was right, he was a coward, but it was even worse than that. He purposefully guided his attacks to hit the parts of her body that would be hidden. It was not young passion in the heat of an angry moment. It was sustained. It was pre-meditated. It was evil.

The cold fear that gripped her as she stepped across the threshold into what should have been her happy marital home was always stifling, particularly because each market day she would make the active decision to return to a situation that she knew could not last. The fear of divorce and letting everyone down paralyzed her, and was

compounded by the reality that she truly tried to hide from herself –
she was absolutely terrified of her husband.

Her eyes adjusting from the bright sunny day to dark interior of her
entryway hid from immediate view the hand that shot out and grabbed
her by the shoulder of her dress and dragged her body completely into
shadow before the front door slammed and clicked. Unfortunately, the
temporarily blindness did nothing to cushion the blow as her husband's
knuckles struck her left cheek, sending her spinning and hitting the
inside of the doorway with her right cheek . She saw lights and felt pain,
unlike anything that she had ever felt, even at his hand. Pain and shock
silenced any instinctive cry that should have come.

"You continue to bring this on yourself, my darling." His voice was
cold and quiet.

She reached out to steady herself on the wall and the side of her
face that had just hit the wall suddenly took another blow from his
knuckles, harder than the fist, sending her body plummeting to the
ground. She had enough time to wonder what in the world she could
have done to bring on such a violent attack when the blows started
coming again. She could not focus on anything with her eyes as his
fists and feet made contact after contact, blow after blow. The sickening
sound of solid parts of his body, slamming into the delicate skin and
flesh of her body sounded in an almost continuous refrain, as he
unleashed unimaginable brutality on her. Maybe she cried out and
maybe not. She couldn't be sure, as he never allowed her a moment
to get her bearings or catch her breath. At some point the torment
became incessant and she no longer felt each individual blow. Vaguely
she realized that there was a crack and then another, but by that point,
she didn't feel the cause distinctly.

After a time, she did not know if it was long or short, she became
aware that the actual new hits had stopped. She twisted her head to
look up, not having the strength to lift her head. The light coming
through the window behind his head put Walter in silhouette, but she

could tell that he used a cloth to wipe his hands as he stared down at her. "You are such a disappointment as a wife, Rachel," he said calmly. "Did you really think that I wouldn't know that you traipse off every week to see Samuel at the market like a common whore?" He crouched down and tilted his head as he looked at her. "Now your face is ugly enough to match who you are." He spit on the rag that he was using to wipe his hands and reached out to roughly smear it across her cheek. You have some blood on your face. Get cleaned up before I come home for dinner." And with that he stood and casually excited the house, closing the front door behind him.

As soon as the door clicked, Rachel's tears started. The pain was insurmountable. She couldn't move and when she tried, sharp pain shot through her ribs. She knew that her face was swelling up because it started getting harder to blink. She gave up on her attempts to stand and simply rested her head on the ground, wondering distantly if he would kill her when he came home to an empty kitchen, before she passed out completely.

Rachel was woken sometime later by a knocking on the door. As she came to, pain lanced through so many parts of her body at once that she could not even distinguish them all. She did her best to breathe through her nose to prevent the vomit that was pushing at the back of her throat from coming up. The disorientation was profound, as her muddled mind struggled to figure out where she was and why she hurt so badly. It all came back to her in a rush of confusion and terror. Walter had almost killed her. She did not know how long she had been there on the floor, but there was still light coming through the windows, which was good. Walter never returned home before the sun had set.

The knocking got louder and a deep voice called out, "Mrs. Webber, are you there?"

She did not have the strength to answer or move, and hoped that whoever that was would come in and help her up, or she would likely die where she lay.

The door opened slowly and stopped against the bag of food from the market that lay discarded on the floor next to her. "Mrs. Webber? It's Amos Bayler, your neighbor."

She tried to speak but it came out as a choked cry. It was loud enough though, that he obviously heard it, because his head peaked around the door. As soon as he saw her his eyes widened and he rushed over to her, lowering himself to his knees next to her twisted form.

"Mrs. Webber, my God." He gently, but firmly untwisted her limbs and helped her lay more comfortably, if there was such a thing when a body was as broken as hers. "I need to leave you for a moment to get some help," he said, starting to stand.

"Please, wait," she croaked out with intense effort. He lowered himself back down and leaned in to hear her better. "Not my husband."

He opened his mouth, likely to ask why. But then his eyes first widened in understanding and then narrowed in anger. With a curt nod, he stood and said in a gentle voice, not matching the ferocity on his face, "I will be back in a minute."

Rachel didn't know why, but despite the pain and vulnerability of that moment, she felt safe having Amos Bayler there. She let herself succumb and the world around her went black.

* * *

When Rachel came to, she was in a strange place. The air was cold, but her body was under warm blankets. There were beeping sounds and a whooshing sound that she recognized as an air conditioner from the times that she had been in other office buildings or stores. Still disoriented, she tried to sit up and groaned. Her entire body hurt and she realized there were ropes attached to her body, pulling on her hands and nose. Suddenly panicked, she pushed herself up through the pain and started to pull at the ropes.

"Rachel, wait." A man's deep voice froze her efforts. She knew it wasn't Walter's voice because even though it was deep, it was gentle.

Walter always spoke with a harsh scowl on his face when he addressed her. There was never any of the compassion and concern that she heard in this person's voice. Looking up, she realized that the voice belonged to the handsome neighbor that she had never dared speak to in fear of retribution from her husband.

"Amos Bayler. What are you doing here? What are these ropes?"

"Rachel, you're at the hospital. Do you remember at all what happened to you today?" He took a few tentative steps forward as he spoke.

Suddenly a woman in bright purple scrubs, whom she didn't recognize, entered the room with a clipboard and started reading the beeping machines and taking down notes. She began fiddling with the ropes, which Rachel now recognized as being IV lines. "Hello, honey. How are you feeling?" She busied herself with more notes and charts.

"I hurt a lot."

The woman's eyes were kind. "I know you do, sweetie. Just lay back and rest. Here, let me adjust the bed a bit for you." Once she was sure that Rachel was comfortable, she said "I'll be back in a few minutes with something for the pain and I think that the hospital social worker is going to want to speak with you when you feel a bit stronger. "

"Okay, thank you," Rachel said, overwhelmed by waking up in such a foreign place.

"Amos, I don't recognize that nurse. What hospital is this?"

"I brought you to Central." He held his hands up like he was worried that she would be angry, and he was surrendering.

"Central?" She was shocked.

"Why would you go to so much trouble? What happened to me? You've never even spoken to me. My husband is not kind to you." She felt a warm rush of gratitude, eclipsed by that still lingering confusion.

"I just...well, I saw you there on the floor and...do you remember what happened?" He sat down in the chair next to her hospital bed.

He obviously was struggling with what to say to her, and she wanted to know why.

"I remember Walter being angry. I remember...well, he lost his temper like I've never seen him do before." Amos' eyes were hard and he nodded, but did not comment. "Then I remember...you. You, like an angel to save me. And then everything went black."

"I was coming over to borrow a tool. I had seen your husband leave and hadn't had time to catch him. But I figured that you would be able to give it to me. I was working on something for the elders and they suggested I borrow it. And that's when I found you there on the ground."

"I'm sorry," she said, suddenly overwhelmed with the understanding of what that must have been like for him.

He closed his eyes and took a deep breath. When he opened them again, his eyes were nearly black. "Please do not ever again apologize to me for what your gutless husband has done to you. He deserves more than what will come to him. And that I know to be true."

Amos was angry. Rachel could tell that, but for some reason it did not scare her the way that it did when Walter was angry. "I can trust you," she simply stated.

"Yes, you can," was his simple reply.

They sat in silence for a few minutes. She closed her eyes and rested against the pillows, taking stock of what hurt in her body. Her ribs on her left side were throbbing and it hurt all over her torso to take a deep breath. Her limbs felt like they had been seen a fall of a cliff or a buggy accident. And her face stung and throbbed at the same time. She couldn't see clearly out of her left eye. She wondered if there was any internal damage. Flashes of memory from the beating started to cross her mind. She had never thought him capable of losing control the way that he had. He was always so controlled in his abuse, so deliberate. This had been passionate, evil in a different way. He wanted to kill her. What could have possibly have provoked such a reaction? And then, suddenly, she remembered. Samuel. Walter had called her a whore for speaking to her friend. And suddenly it was too much, and she cried. She cried, and then sobbed for what seemed like forever. Amos put his hand out for her to hold, and it became her lifeline. She gasped for air through her tears, as shooting pain jabbed at her ribs.

They sat like that for a long time, even after her tears had subsided. She half expected Walter to come crashing through the door demanding to know why she was holding this man's hand, but strangely enough, that did not scare her as much as it probably should have. Amos made her feel safe and cared for, something that her husband had never done for her.

"Amos," she said after a long stretch of silence.

"Yes?"

"Why did you take me to Central instead of the village hospital?" She had never had anyone go out of their way like that, and she was still having trouble comprehending why. She was always the one that went above and beyond for other people, not the other way around.

"I just wanted to give you some privacy. There are going to be questions about where you've gone, but there would be so many more about what had happened to you if you were in the village hospital. As you heard, they are obligated to get the social workers and possibly police involved, so that would mean that the entire village would know what was happening to you. It is nothing to be ashamed of, at least for you. Walter should be very ashamed. But I wanted to give you the chance to figure out how you want to approach this with your family and the community." He paused, and added in a slightly less gentle tone, "And I know that you care so much about the community and what they think."

Without knowing why, the last part of his statement bothered Rachel. "Why do you say I care about the community and what it thinks like it's is a bad thing?"

"Oh, Rachel, it's not a bad thing most of the time. But you do it at the expense of your own health and safety. You have been putting on a pretense, I suspect since your marriage started, that all is well and you are the perfect wife and community member. What has he been doing, hiding his abuse purposefully? Has he been intentionally hurting you under where your dress would sit? That is insane." His voice got more and more forceful as he ranted. And by the end he was standing, breathing heavily and running his hands through his hair.

Suddenly feeling a twinge of fear, Rachel said, "Amos, please calm down. You're scaring me."

His eyes went wide and he immediately sat down again, an apology written all over his face. "Oh, Rachel, I'm such a fool. I'm so sorry. If you would like me to leave, please just tell me."

"No," she practically shouted at him. "Please don't leave, unless you want to."

"I don't want to. I'll stay with you until it's time to go home, if that is what you need. No one should ever be alone, and I will make sure that you stay safe."

What he did not say was that he would keep her safe from Walter, should be bother to show his face at the hospital. Although, he was a complete coward, and leaving the community would mean that he would be unprotected, and he would never allow that to happen when all of his power was from preying on the weak.

There was a knock on the door and a small blond woman in a streamlined navy dress click-clacked her heels into the room. "Mrs. Webber?" Her voice was all business, but not unkind.

"Yes." She hated the last name. It made the hair on the back of her neck stand on end.

"My name is Shelia Winter. I am a social worker here at Central Hospital. I work specifically with women and children that come to the hospital with injuries consistent with physical abuse." She looked at Amos with loathing on her face. "Are *you* Mr. Webber?"

"No I'm not. If I was, you would never be needed for this woman."

"This is Amos Bayler, a good friend. He is the one that found me and brought me to the hospital outside of our village. He wanted to keep me safe." She realized that she was staring at him as she spoke, and blushed.

Ms. Winter's tone softened noticeably. "Well, Mr. Bayler, you did a wonderful thing. Thank you. May I ask for a few minutes alone to speak with Mrs. Webber?"

"Sure." Amos started to stand.

"No, wait," she said to Amos. She looked at Ms. Winter. "I would like him to stay if that is possible."

Ms. Winter looked between the two f them. "Okay. Just a quick question to ask you both upfront: is this a romantic relationship? Could that be the catalyst for this situation? Not that it will make a difference. I just need to know as much as I can about the particulars."

"No, she said. Today is the first time that we have ever spoken, Ms. Winter."

"Well, okay then," she said with a smile. "Have a seat, Mr. Bayler. Let's get started and see what we can do for you, Mrs. Webber."

* * *

That night, when visiting hours were over, the nurses finally had to ask Amos to leave. He stayed until the last possible moment. And for the next two weeks, Rachel stayed in the hospital recovering from what the police had said was one of the worst beatings that they had seen in a domestic dispute in many years. During that time she was never alone. Either Amos, Samuel or her family members were there.

The day before she was leave the hospital, her mother sat in the corner chair doing needle point as Rachel read a book.

"Your bruises are looking so much better, my love," her mother said.

"My ribs are much better too. I just have to be careful when I move around."

"I want to say something to you, Rachel."

"Okay, go ahead." She was nervous about what she was going to hear, as her mother did not typically start off conversations in this manner.

"I'm so sorry." Tears pooled in her mother's eyes as she looked at her.

"Mom, what are you talking about?"

"I pushed you to marry Walter Webber. I ignored the signs that you weren't happy. I ignored the signs that you were suffering physically. I fed you with the idea that divorce is for weak, selfish women, without ever really considering how it would hurt you. I judged and I talked about things that I didn't understand. And I led you to this."

"No, mom, this is not your fault."

"We may have to agree to disagree on that point, my love." She put up her hand up as Rachel opened her mouth to argue again. "All I want to say is that I want you to divorce that monster as soon as possible. And we will help you, as will our Samuel, and your angel, Amos Bayler."

Rachel nodded, unable to speak. This was the deliverance from guilt and further suffering that she needed. Her mother understood. The community would have to understand if her mother did. She suspected that Amos had something to do with her mother's change of heart, but she didn't want to ruin the moment. Instead she decided to broach the subject that she had been avoiding for weeks. "Mom, why haven't I heard from Walter?"

Her mother gave up a sigh and shook her head. "Darling, Walter has been missing since the day that Amos brought you here to Central. The police believe that there is the possibility that foul play is involved because no one, not even his family, or his...um, friends...have heard from him."

"Mom, were going to say his girlfriend?"

Her mom looked shocked, but sighed again. "Did you know the whole time?"

"I suspected, but was too afraid to ask, for fear of his reaction."

"I'm so sorry, darling."

"Please don't. And please don't tell me who it was. I don't want to know."

Her mom nodded and said, "As you wish, my love. Let's not talk about him again for now. We can deal with this when you come home.

* * *

When Rachel returned to her community from the hospital, she decided that the best thing would be for her to return to her parents' home. The word that she received was that Walter was still missing, but she didn't want to take any chances with her safety. She was much recovered, but nowhere near strong enough to survive any abuse at his hand again. Having her mother's support and the protection of both Samuel and Amos made her feel slightly more comfortable returning to the village, but she was still scared. She had been beaten and left for dead on the floor of her own entryway. That was not something that she would soon forget.

It had not even been an hour after her return, when there was a knock at her mother's door. Rachel froze. The fear that the caller could be her husband overwhelmed her senses. Her mother quickly walked to and opened the front door. "Good afternoon." It was a man's voice, but not one that she recognized.

"Hello, how may I help you," her mother said.

"Detective John Styles of Farmington PD. I am looking for Mrs. Rachel Webber and was told that she was returning here today from Central Hospital." He spoke fast and his voice was rough with an edge of a smoker's rasp.

"I'm Rachel Webber," Rachel said loudly as she stood from her seat and made her way through the room to meet her mother at the front door. "What can I do for you, Detective?"

"I would like to speak with you about your husband, Walter Webber. May I come in?"

"Actually, why don't I come outside so that my mother can continue on with her work? There is a nice set of seats on the porch." She had no intention of letting this man into her mother's home. The community did not look favorably upon outsiders coming in to their village, and outside law enforcement, while allowed to enter and conduct business as they needed to, was not always a welcomed sight.

"Alright." He stepped back, allowing her to pass and she led him to a seat. She sat next to him and waited. "Mrs. Webber, I received a full report from the hospital about the injuries you suffered, as well as your and Mr. Bayler's versions of events. I am very sorry for your suffering."

Rachel bristled a bit at this, because he did not actually sound the least bit sorry. But she kept her comments to herself and nodded, urging him to continue.

"We have not gotten your husband's version of events."

"My understanding is that he has been missing since the day that he attacked me."

"That is no longer the case Mrs. Webber."

Her skin prickled and she spoke softly, "so you have found my husband then?"

"Yes ma'am. How long were you in the hospital?"

"Just over two weeks. Why?"

"Did you ever wonder during that time why your husband never came to see you?"

"With all due respect, Detective, if someone attacked you, would you be eager to see them again?"

"Fair point, ma'am. But that doesn't change the fact that it was strange. Was it not?"

"I just figured that he either didn't care or didn't want to deal with law enforcement outside of the village, where he is away from the community protection. What is this line of questioning about, sir?

Because I know that you have better things to do than come all the way out to the village on a muddy Tuesday afternoon to ask what I think about my husband's lack of respect for me."

The detective nodded, acknowledging her point. "Well, ma'am, it is just that we have found your husband. Or rather I should say, your husband's body."

"I'm sorry?"

"Your husband's body was discovered in the woods, off of a hiking trail early this morning. He has been dead for quite some time. We don't know the cause of death yet, but will be putting a rush on an autopsy and tox screen."

"Oh my." It was the only thing that she could will herself to say. Her head was muddled because the reality was that she was not entirely unhappy to hear the news.

"Do you know of anyone that might want to harm your husband?"

"Sorry?"

"I have been speaking to some of your neighbors, and they seem to think that your friend Samuel Wills is not a particularly big fan of your husband. Would you concur?"

"Would you like the person that was beating your best friend?"

He continued on as if he had not heard her. "And Mr. Amos Bayler. I understand that he happened upon you a few hours after the alleged assault."

"Alleged?"

"Well we do not have any witnesses beside the two of you to corroborate the stories, so I cannot place blame on an assailant at this point."

"Did you not see the pictures? I was beaten to a bloody pulp."

"Yes, Mrs. Webber. And I mean no disrespect here, but you cannot prove that your husband is the one that did that to you?"

She was stunned. He must have been kidding.

He continued on, pretending that he had not just accused a domestic assault victim of lying. "And you, Mrs. Webber, what about you?"

"What about me?"

"Yes. Did you want to hurt your husband?"

"What are you saying?"

"Well, you claim that your husband was out of control, yes?"

"Yes."

"Then, again, no disrespect, but why are you alive? From the way you describe it, he was acting as if he had no control over his behavior at that time. Why did he stop before he killed you?"

Rachel could not believe what she was hearing. There was no way that this was happening to her.

"I'm going to offer you an alternative scenario, Mrs. Webber. Perhaps you were having an affair with Mr. Amos. Perhaps you two plotted and carried out the murder of your husband and then staged a beating to make it look like he had done something horrible to you to remove suspicion. What do you think of that?"

"I think that you have been reading too many crime novels, Detective. And if you have nothing further to accuse me of, I suggest that you leave and come back with some proof or evidence supporting your wild theory."

"Fair enough. Don't' leave town, Mrs. Webber. This is not over."

After the Detective left, her mother came out the door. Her face was red and her hands were balled into fists. "So you heard that then," Rachel said. She was numb from the shock of the news and the accusation.

"I most certainly did. I am going to go speak with Samuel and Amos. You rest here, darling, and don't worry about a thing."

"Alright." She shuffled into the house and lay in her bed, not bothering to change out of her day dress. She closed her eyes and wondered vaguely, before drifting off to sleep, if this nightmare would ever end.

Over the next week, Rachel spent her time recovering at home. Her mother, Samuel and Amos, as well as other community members were all very attentive. Word had gotten around about the police accusations, and the community was standing on thin ice, waiting for the results of all of the testing.

"You need a blanket," Amos said to Rachel as they sat together on her mother's porch, one month to the day after the beating that landed her in the hospital.

"Amos, please don't fuss."

"Excuse me, Mrs. Webber?" The familiar smoker's rasp of Detective Styles drew her attention to the bottom of the porch steps.

"Hello Detective. What new theories bring you here today?" She had not meant to be rude, but her anger over the way he had treated her before was something that she wasn't capable of hiding.

Amos moved closer to her side, putting a protective hand on Rachel's shoulder. The gesture was not lost on the detective, and he continued on.

"Mrs. Webber, I and the Farmington PD would like to issue you a formal apology. Your husband drank himself into his grave. He was severely intoxicated when he died, and for whatever reason he was all the way out there, he passed out from the drink and succumbed to exposure."

"So that's it? You just issue a weak apology and expect us to trust you here in our village." Amos' voice was hard, but his touch on her should remained gentle and reassuring.

"Mr. Bayler, please believe that I am sorry for the way that the case was handled at the beginning, but I needed to be sure."

"You made a mistake and jumped the gun. I think..."

"Amos, please. Just let it go. All is fine and I don't want to think about Walter anymore. Detective, thank you for delivering the news, but now please vacate the premises and don't return to my home unless it is to save, rather than ruin someone. "

The detective looked genuinely chagrinned. He pulled some paperwork and then was on his way.

"Phew," said Amos. I was wondering when he was going to leave."

"Why?" She gasped when she looked up, as his face was right there, moving toward her. "What are you..."

But his lips were on her and his hands caressed her as if she were something sacred. She should have been scared. It should have felt awkward, but it didn't. She gave in and returned the kiss. She had a new, braver heart, born of the suffering that she had endured. In her head she thought to herself, "My new heart can now lead me to a new start. She smiled against his lips and leaned her body closer. It was time to enjoy a life without fear, suffering, or guilt. Amos had saved her life in more ways than one. Now she wanted to discover what real love could be, and she knew that she would find it with him.

The Mysterious Englischer

Erica Hennig

Emma Queener wasn't sure what to make of the new face standing in front of her. His red hair, green eyes, and freckled skin said he was certainly of Irish descent, but he claimed his name was John Smith.

"A phone book isn't exactly the best way to look me up," he chuckled and smiled shyly at her, trying to make light of the already tense situation.

"So, are you staying in town for the night?" Emma worked in the shop on the edge of her little Amish community and always thought of herself as the first line of defense against any strange outsiders. Mr. Smith seemed to fit that description very well.

"Oh no. I'll be moving into town. I'm going to be living in that quaint little house right across the street." He pointed at the Troyer's house.

"You'll be living with the Troyer's?" Emma was more than wary of this strange newcomer. In fact, she simply didn't feel right about him. As his smile faltered a bit, any sense of security she may have felt dissipated in that moment. She desperately wished her brother would come from the back to stand beside her.

"Ah, I'm sorry. No. You know, all of these houses look so similar here." He began digging in the bag he had been carrying and Emma instinctively jumped back. In response, Mr. Smith quickly removed his hand with nothing in it.

"Whoa," he exclaimed as Emma's brother Evan suddenly appeared with fire in his eyes and a surety Emma had never heard in his voice.

"I think you need to leave," Evan declared.

"I'm sorry, I'm just—"

"Now!"

With a final glance at Emma and a nod in Evan's direction, John Smith left the store.

"Are you okay?" Evan asked as soon as he was gone. He grabbed Emma by the shoulders tenderly and pulled her into a hug. Being the youngest of five children, Emma tended to be the most trusting and always found the best in people, but something about the newcomer really struck her.

"Why did he scare me, Brother?" Emma asked as she pulled away from Evan's hug after a moment.

He shook his head. "I wish I knew. You're the last person I would expect to be scared of someone." He ran a hand through his sandy hair.

Emma looked out toward the door and saw the stranger walking around aimlessly, as if he legitimately couldn't find what he was looking for.

"Maybe he really is lost." Without thinking, she made for the door.

"Emma, wait!" Evan was on her heels trying to stop her, but she was already out the door and too close to John Smith for him to pull her back.

"Sir?" Emma decided that no matter how much he scared her, she was still going to be nice. "Are you really lost?"

He looked at the paper in his hands before looking back at the siblings. He simply nodded. Emma looked at Evan and he simply sighed.

"Where are you trying to go?"

That night the Queener family were eager to know of Emma and Evan's experience with the new man in town. They were the only people to make any contact since he arrived and the whole town wanted some hint of who this man was.

"At first he seemed really cryptic, almost like he had never done this before," Emma began. "It made more sense when he told us he just recently left the Englisher lifestyle."

"But he didn't tell us *why,*" Evan interjected. "And that makes him dangerous."

Their mother, Mary Queener, was quick to add her thoughts: "Maybe he's just unsure of what to do. We must be patient with him and do everything we can to make him feel welcome."

"Mama, he said 'quaint.'" Evan gave his mother an exasperated look. "What grown man do you know that uses that word in a sentence?"

Emma and her older sister Emily giggled as Emma added, "I forgot about that part." Emma grew serious. "What scares me the most is that he goes by a very general name: John Smith." She looked at her father. "Should I be scared of him, Papa?"

Esau Queener looked at each of the children seated at the table—Emily, Evan, and finally Emma—before answering.

"I think you should be careful with everyone you meet. However, that doesn't mean you don't show them the same mercy you would want if you suddenly left everything you knew in an instant. We must remember where he came from, he is an Englisher. What do we do with Englishers?"

Everyone seemed too afraid to answer the question until finally Mary cleared her throat and answered, "We treat them like anyone else." Esau smiled at his wife, glad that somebody responded.

"Yes. Yes we do. Because Jesus Christ didn't discriminate between Jew or Gentile. He died for all of them. So we must show everyone the light of the world and what He can do for them."

The three children seemed thoughtful as they finished their meal in silence. Emma and Emily asked to be excused so they could finish their chores before going to bed. Evan seemed content to stay back and talk to Mama and Papa for a little while longer. Since he was the only boy left in the house, his responsibilities were changing. And Emily was in a relationship with Thomas Troyer, the cutest boy in the community, even by Emma's high standards. Emma was eager to hear about what strides he had been making to win her sister's heart.

"Oh, we didn't do anything too crazy today," Emily said with a wave of her hand. "We just hung out with his little sister most of the day."

"Which one? Hope?" Emma already knew the answer because Hope didn't love spending time with people so much as she was extremely protective of her older brother. Emily giggled.

"Of course. I think his parents just let her come along to make sure we don't do any 'hanky panky.'" The girls giggled until they heard movement in the next room. They hurried to finish the dishes so they could get ready for bed and chat a little more. Emily loved sharing with Emma and Emma loved to hear the stories.

She always claimed to be a hopeless romantic, and she lived up to that name quite often. Emma had only been asked to court by one guy in the entire community, and that was because that guy had gotten her confused with her oldest sister Martha. It was an awkward date anyway, Emma would tell everyone, but deep down she wished someone would pay attention to her like that young man did until he realized he had the wrong girl.

Maybe one day, my love will find me, she thought to herself as she drifted off to sleep.

The community became more intrigued by the stranger as the days went on, the biggest reason being that nobody ever saw him. He would come to church on Sundays and he would shop once a week, usually on Mondays. Eventually Emma found herself defending him to the members of the community.

"I don't trust him," some would say. "He hides in his house all day, but somehow manages to keep his yard looking tidy. I think it's witchcraft."

"He must go out when no one is around to see him," Emma would say. "I'm pretty sure he's not a witch."

"How do you know? Does he talk to you?"

"As a matter of fact, he does. He comes in every week and has a conversation with me and Evan. Isn't that right, Evan?"

But Evan would never admit to speaking with the stranger and Emma couldn't understand why that was. Eventually people started to think that Emma might have feelings for the man. Though she denied it, deep down she could feel something that didn't used to be there. This was the first man ever who had shown any interest in Emma, however brief their conversations might be. God worked in mysterious ways... maybe John Smith was the man she had been waiting for.

One Sunday evening during the hymnal singing and fellowship, John Smith showed up. Emma guessed it was because he was lonely and immediately made her way to him. She could feel eyes staring at her, wondering what she was doing with the outsider. She could hear the whispers of those whom she had considered friends, condescension in their quiet tones as she made her way to John and looked him in the eye. Despite the giggles and "Emma's in love" claims that she could no longer deny, she smiled at the man before her. Slowly, he smiled back.

"The people here suddenly don't seem to like you," he whispered to her. She shrugged.

"Let them think what they will. Man's opinions don't matter, it's what Gott thinks about a man." John seemed surprised by this response, but said nothing. Instead he changed the subject and asked where Emma was sitting. She obliged the subject change and showed her new friend the table where she was seated.

He seemed to do all the right things: he was very cordial and sweet. He said all the right things: he knew about Gott and the Plain way of living. But something about his tone, something about the way he looked at those around him... Emma could finally see that he was hiding something.

Maybe he's just nervous, she thought. *This is his first time coming after all. We'll see how he does next week.*

Sure enough, in the weeks that followed, he seemed to become more comfortable. The young people began accepting John Smith as one of their own, and by proxy, the rest of the community started opening their doors to John a little more. As soon as this happened, people began to see John out and about. He would come outside at different times of the day and talk with the neighbors. He would go to the community workdays, and go over to people's houses for dinner. Emma was pleased that people were finally accepting John as a member of the community, as well as teaching him the finer points of living in a Plain community. He seemed to be fitting in really well...

And then tragedy struck.

Thomas Troyer ran into the store so fast, he nearly knocked over a fruit display that Emma had just finished setting up.

"Where's Hope?" He practically charged the counter as if expecting to find her hiding behind the counter.

"Not here," Emma furrowed her brow. "Where's Emily?"

"Out looking for Hope!" There was desperation in the young Troyer's eyes. "We're *all* looking for Hope." He paused. When he spoke again, his voice was barely above a whisper. "She didn't come home last night."

Emma froze. Hope Troyer wasn't the kind of girl to be out much past sundown. The exceptions were if she was with someone, but she was always sure someone knew who she would be with.

"Did she say anything last night?" At that moment, Evan came from the back of the store.

"What's going on?"

"It's Hope. She's missing." Evan's face registered shock.

"*What?*"

"Evan, you have to help us find my sister!" Thomas interjected himself back into the conversation as if Emma and Evan didn't know he was still there. But they couldn't ignore the crazed look and panicked presence he carried.

"Okay, I will Thomas." Evan remained calm, but Emma wondered what he would be like if any of his sisters suddenly went missing. Would he be as frantic as Thomas, or even more?

"Where have you all looked? Who's looking?" Emma wanted to know some logistics so that she didn't tread over ground that had already been covered.

"This was the last building, except for John Smith's house."

"But he lives right next door," Evan pointed out. "Why not go there first?"

Thomas's face darkened. "My father thinks it was him."

Emma and Evan exchanged shocked glances. "If there's one thing John is, it's certainly not a kidnapper."

"No, but he could be a killer. What do we really know about him? Nothing, so stop sticking up for him." He pointed at each of them. "Both of you. Now, are you going to help or not?"

The answer was of course, that they would help. Evan left with Thomas to go talk to John while Emma closed up the store. When she arrived at John's house less than ten minutes later, the scene was anything but calm. Thomas had resorted to screaming at John while he just stood there like a stone, his face becoming increasingly more red. Evan looked confused as to what to do, so as soon as Emma was close enough, she put herself between the two men.

"Hey!"

They looked at her.

"Emma—"

She silenced her brother with a gesture.

"There is a girl missing." She looked between them and spoke as calmly as possible, even though the storm inside of her just wanted to yell at everybody. "I understand that you are both upset for various reasons, but what evidence do either of you have to resort to being children?"

John simply put his head down, and Thomas sighed heavily. After a few moments, he finally broke his glare on the red-haired man and looked at Emma.

"I just want to find my sister." He broke down and began to weep. Evan pulled him off toward the Troyer's residence, leaving John and Emma standing alone on his porch.

She looked at him and sighed. "I'm really sorry about this." He shook his head.

"Don't be. If it were my sister, the first person I would suspect would be the one I trust the least. I haven't been the most forthcoming about my past either... but you can trust me when I say I had nothing to do with this."

Emma looked in his eyes, unsure of his sincerity. "I'd like to believe you, but I simply can't right now." She looked away, suddenly aware of what she had just said. "I'm sorry."

He shook his head in exasperation. "Guilty until proven innocent around here, huh?" Without any further explanation or warning, he slammed the door in her face. In that moment, Emma suddenly felt guilty for the lack of faith she had just shown in someone she had helped the whole town learn to trust. How could she lead them to trust someone she didn't even trust? What if he really did do it, and she was protecting a kidnapper and potential killer?

She felt as if she had been punched in the gut with the sudden thought that Hope could be dead. Were there others in danger? Was *she* in danger? She began running home. She heard Evan calling her, asking what she was doing, but she just needed some safety. The one place she knew was safe was next to her parents, but when she arrived there, breathless and tired from running, only Emily was there. She looked up from the chair she was in, tears in her eyes. All sadness vanished when she noticed her little sister's worried look.

"What if he's after us?" Emma asked before Emily could ask what was wrong.

Emily rose from her seat and met Emma in the doorway, drawing her into a hug. With that hug came a flood of emotions Emma didn't even know she had. All of the fear, sadness, curiosity, and anxiety came bubbling over and she completely collapsed in her sister's embrace.

"I don't want to die," she managed to speak between sobs. Emily pulled her back and looked her in the eyes.

"Hey! You're not going to die. You're safe here. Nothing will happen to you, do you hear me? You are safe. Gott has you in His wings, just like He carries Hope and just like He carries all of His children. Trust Him."

Emma eventually nodded. Her sister was right and she knew it.

"Now," Emily said as Emma calmed down. "We need to find out what we can do to help."

It wasn't long before news spread throughout the entire community: Hope was missing and the newcomer was holed up in his house. Because John was still so new, many of the members began to suspect he was holding Hope in his house. They weren't about to give up as quickly as Emma had.

Emma retreated into herself. She didn't want to help and she didn't want to find Hope. She didn't want to be a good person and stand up for John Smith anymore. She didn't want to trust Gott or do or say anything that had to do with Gott. Emily said Gott was protecting Hope, but Emma had this horrible feeling that Hope was no longer alive.

Despite all of Emily's attempts to get Emma back out to help with the search and rescue, Emma opted to stay home and clean. Cleaning helped clear her mind and forced her to think in a forward motion.

If Hope is still alive, what kind of state will she be in? I'll need to be a friend more than ever. What if she's not alive? What do the Troyer's need?

And then it came to her. She would help to organize meals for the Troyer's. Regardless of if Hope was alive or not, people still needed to eat. She finished what she was doing and quickly left the house to find someone to share her idea with. She saw a large group of people at the church. Something was wrong, she could tell. Her stomach instantly knotted. Evan spotted her coming and ran out to meet her.

"Emma, I just have to let you know... you're not going to like it." She gave her brother a look and continued toward the church, pushing people out of the way as she got closer to the epicenter. Then she heard it. It started out small and grew in intensity. A cry, no more than a cry. It was a wail. It stretched on for a few seconds before being joined by others. Emma finally saw Hope. Her lifeless body was lying on the steps of the church, Mrs. Troyer was holding her head and rocking.

"My baby! My baby!"

The world around Emma disappeared. All the preparation in the world wouldn't have helped her in that moment. How could this happen? Emma couldn't think. She didn't even realize she had moved away from Hope and Mrs. Troyer until her brother was holding her and telling her to breathe. She remembered telling him she needed to get home, and then nothing.

Emma woke with a start. She quickly sat up. She looked around. She was in her living room, her father was in his chair reading by candlelight and her mother was sewing. Was the whole day a dream? Did she just wake up from a bad dream?

"What happened?" Her parents both looked up at her. Mary had tears in her eyes and quickly covered her mouth to silence a sob. Esau simply looked at her lovingly and smiled.

Emma knew then that what had happened was not a dream.

"It's getting late my dear," her father spoke after a minute. "Would you like some dinner?" He rose from his chair and made his way to the kitchen. As Emma threw off the blanket that had been placed on her, she remembered her idea for meals for the Troyer's. She decided to ask her mother about the idea.

"Well," Mary's voice was shaky. "I think that would be a great idea, honey. Would you like some assistance?" Emma nodded. "Well let's talk while you eat."

While they were eating, Emma thought only of Hope. "I know this is hard... but where did they find her?"

Both parents looked at each other with worried looks. "In the woods, less than half a mile from John Smith's house."

For the second time that day, Emma suddenly felt queasy. She pushed her food away, barely untouched. "Maybe it's not a good idea that I eat," she finally admitted. "Mama, I'm scared." She looked up at her mother, both of their eyes swimming with tears.

Papa spoke slowly and clearly, "I can't guarantee that anyone will be completely safe. We live in a fallen world. But I can promise that I will do all I can to keep you as safe as I can. As long as you live under my roof, no harm will come to you." He looked at his wife and youngest child with an intensity that Emma had never seen before.

And then there was a knock at the door.

Everyone froze. Emma was afraid to even breathe. Finally, Esau rose to answer. From the kitchen Emma and her mother could hear the door open and Esau's low voice, though they couldn't make out the words. In fact, they didn't even hear another voice, but then Esau was in the kitchen again.

"Honey," he began as if it was the last thing he was going to say. Mary began to shake, as if afraid that her husband may not make it through the night. "There's someone here. He wants us to protect him. He's afraid, and he's a person just like us. He's—"

"John!" Emma saw him peek around her father's shoulder briefly. Sleeping for as long as she had must have helped the way she felt, because she didn't feel as unsure about him as she had earlier.

The way she reacted surprised both men and they exchanged glances.

"Hi, Emma," John came around Esau and accepted the hug that Emma extended.

"I'm so sorry for what I said to you earlier. I—" He waved a hand and stopped her mid sentence.

"If I were in your situation, I would've done the same thing. I come from the English world, I've never explained myself, et cetera." He paused and smiled. "Trust me, the last thing I'm thinking about were some words you said to me while you were upset." He moved into the room and sat down at an empty chair.

"I think it's time I tell you all my story. Emma has proven that she can be trusted and I know she gets that from you. Are Evan and Emily asleep? I want them to hear this as well."

Mary ran off to get Emma's two older siblings while Emma sat down. *Maybe I should try to eat before he tells his story,* she thought. Esau sat heavily while Emma forced a few bites of food into her mouth. In another minute, Evan and Emily were up and Mary was making everyone tea to drink.

"This will be an interesting story," Evan quipped.

John started his story by telling them his real name: Liam O'Shaughnessy.

"I would have picked John Smith if I was moving away from my old life too," Emily joked.

"Actually, I'm an undercover FBI agent searching for a serial killer. He's been going after girls about the same age, height, and look as Hope. In fact, he's been so evasive because he's only been hitting these types of communities. In the last community I was in, I got so involved in the community that they actually excommunicated me when I told them I was an FBI agent. That's why I've been so secretive about my life. I want to appear as normal as possible."

"Have you found any clues that would cause you to think the killer is still here?"

"The killer actually lives here," Liam said matter-of-factly. "The way he killed the other girls showed that he had no real remorse for what he was doing. When he killed Hope..." Liam chose his words carefully. "He did it as though he knew her well. As though he wished he didn't have to."

"But he doesn't have to," Emily interjected. "He could stop!"

"Well that's the thing about serial killers—they're sociopaths. They have to satiate that desire to kill so badly that nothing else matters." He took a deep breath.

"Have you narrowed down who it could be?" Emma asked, legitimately scared that the killer could be someone she knew.

"I have," Liam said gravely.

It seemed as if the entire room was holding its breath, waiting for him to reveal who he thought it was.

"Backup will be here in the morning. Then we'll begin our official investigations. For tonight, I would like to stay here. I will sleep on the couch, if you don't mind."

Emma's parents helped get Liam set up in the living room while the children went to bed.

"Who do you think it could be?" Emily asked as she snuggled back into the bed across from Emma's. Emma simply shrugged.

"I don't know, but I'm really hoping it's not someone I know really well."

Emily snuggled deeper under her covers and drifted off to sleep in a matter of seconds. Emma wasn't so fortunate. She stayed up a long time staring out into the night sky and listening to her sister snore.

At some point, she realized that Hope looked a lot like she could have been a Queener. A single thought came into her mind: she was next.

She jumped when there was a small knock at the door. She snuck over and opened the door quietly to see Evan standing there. He looked pale, as if he had just seen a ghost. Emma's sisterly instincts took over and she asked him what was wrong.

"Can we go on a walk?" Without hesitation, she grabbed a shawl and left the room, closing the door ever so quietly behind her. "We'll have to go out the back so we don't wake John up."

"You mean Liam," Emma corrected. Evan nodded absentmindedly as they made their way out the back door.

"Thanks for going on a walk with me," Evan said. "After finding out that John Smith isn't really who he led us all to believe, I'm not sure I even believe the story he gave about being an FBI agent."

"I don't know," Emma ventured. "For the first time ever, he seemed really sincere. Maybe we should give him a chance and let him and the FBI do their job."

"No, Emma. You don't understand. There is no mystery here. There is no murderer here. That stuff he gave about how Hope was killed differently than the rest, how does he know that?" Evan stopped walking and looked at Emma. She stopped and they were standing toe-to-toe. "He's a nobody." The look in his eyes was making her uncomfortable, so she turned around to keep walking, but Evan grabbed her by the arm and whirled her around. He pulled her close to him and before she knew what was happening they were kissing! As quickly as she could she pulled away.

"Evan! What is wrong with you?"

"I... I love you, Emma. I don't want to find a wife, because you are the best sister and wife I could ever have. I... I want to be with you."

With every step that Evan took toward her, she took a step back. Without trying, she ended up being sandwiched between a large tree and her brother, who wasn't at all what she thought. Again, he pulled her into him and tried kissing her. He was too strong! She couldn't resist! When she tried to yell for help, he pushed her to the ground, knocking all breath from her lungs. He began to undo his shirt as he knelt down over her. She wasn't sure what was happening but before she had a chance to try to call out for help again, his mouth was on hers.

How did my life get to the point where I was being raped by my brother? She knew there was no fighting it, no one could hear her and they were too far into the woods and in the dark for anyone to see them.

Then she heard it. A twig snapped in the distance. She hoped that it wasn't just a night creature. She began whimpering since she couldn't make any noise with Evan's hand now over her mouth. Instantly he was right next to her ear.

"If you so much as squeak again, I will kill you... just like I did Hope." Tears clouded her vision as he pulled back. He undid his pants and began to pull her dress up as another twig snapped. This time Evan heard it too. He froze in place, while Emma tried her best to not even sniffle. Even if it wasn't a night creature, the last thing Emma wanted was to die. She would remain quiet for as long as she had to, no matter what.

There were no other noises. Evan continued what he was doing, which only brought more tears and fear inside Emma. She knew after this moment, she would never be the same. She closed her eyes trying to keep herself from making any noise. She heard Evan chuckle.

"You always were the most obedient girl I ever knew." She couldn't look at him, unwilling to admit that it was, in fact, her brother committing such a heinous act. A shiver ran through her, partly from the cold and partly from the fear that was coursing through her in that moment.

Emma still had her eyes closed when she heard a THUNK and a body collapse. She opened one eye, mostly out of curiosity. What she saw was one of the most invigorating sights she ever could have seen in that moment. Liam O'Shaughnessy stood over Evan, who was passed out from a hit by what appeared to be a large stick. He was facing away from her.

"Please put your clothes back on and get up. Quickly!" That last part was after Emma continued to sit there in shock. "I need to call this in." Liam looked at her briefly after she finally pulled herself together and got up. He looked concerned. "Are you okay?"

She tried nodding, but instantly her body began shaking from all of the nerves she had been holding. Instantly, he dropped the stick and pulled her into a hug.

He didn't say anything, he just held her. And that's all she needed at that point, a hug.

The next morning there was a flurry of activity between the Queener's and the Troyer's. Now that it had been found out that Evan was the one who had killed Hope, Thomas wanted nothing to do with Emily.

"How could you have not seen this?" Thomas roared at Emily across the street from where Emma was sitting. She watched with all of the sadness in her heart that hadn't already been reserved for Hope or herself. Slowly she rose from where she sat and went over to where they were arguing. Just like she had done the day before with Thomas and Liam, she stood between Thomas and Emily. The differences today were very pointed. Today, Thomas not only stood his ground, but directed more of his anger at Emma than was necessary. Emma—having had no sleep since she woke from her fainting spell last night—had no patience for the man with a short temper. Instead of talking to Thomas, she turned and addressed her sister.

"Emily, this man doesn't deserve you. You are one of the strongest, most loving women I know. If Thomas doesn't see that, then just walk away. Someone else can deal with his temper for the rest of their life." Emily looked hurt, but relieved that someone stood up for her. She smiled and took her little sister's hand. "Let's not lose each other today just because we lost a brother." With that, the Queener sisters walked away, leaving Thomas standing on his side of the street.

He yelled and commanded they come back, but they didn't listen. They were past the point of caring about whiny children posing as adults ready for marriage. At least, that's what Emma thought as they made their way back into the house. The FBI had arrived with the rise of the sun, and with them, all of the gossipers in the little community. Emma had gotten so used to there being whispers around her that they didn't even affect her anymore, but she decided she would be there for her family because they hadn't had to deal with it over the last few months like she had.

She found Liam talking with a fellow agent. "Liam," she decided now was as good a time as any to talk to him. He excused himself from his friend and walked Emma away from the throng of people.

"What's up?" He seemed much more comfortable and simply talked as he normally would, now that there was nothing for him to pretend to be.

"I just wanted to thank you... for saving me." She looked down, suddenly overcome with emotions. *That's not how this was supposed to go!*

Liam pulled her into a side hug. "You're welcome."

"What's going to happen to Evan?" Liam took a deep breath at the question.

"Well," he thought about it for a moment. "He'll be tried in a court and will probably serve a lot of jail time. Regardless of the rights of Amish people, we all still live in America. There is justice to be served."

Emma nodded. "Will you be leaving then?" Liam nodded this time, but more slowly.

"Unfortunately."

"Take me with you." Liam was shocked.

"What?" She looked him in the eye.

"I don't want to be here anymore. There are too many memories of... everything that happened."

"But you're only sixteen. I can't just take you with me. Besides, you still have a family that loves you. They don't need to lose two children today. No. I won't take you... but I will come back and visit until you're legally old enough to leave." He winked and Emma's heart soared.

"I look forward to your next visit," she smiled as he walked away, a small spring in his step.

And she would look forward to his next visit. Even though she lost a brother and a good portion of her innocence, she was excited that she had found some good in it. She had found the one whom her heart loves... and she would wait for him as long as she needed to.

"Emma," Emily came up next to her. "You like him don't you?"

"Even though he scared me at first, I always knew he was a good person. Now I can wait for him because I know that he'll wait for me." Emily looked at her sister.

"Did he really say that?" Emma smiled.

"Did he need to? If I was old enough, he would've taken me with him. That's enough for me." Emily laughed.

"You will always be a hopeless romantic." Emma looked at her sister.

"Am I hopeless if I have a hope though?"

She loved her sister even more in that moment. Now it was just the two of them at home. From now on, they would help to be a light to the community amidst what happened to Hope and to Evan. They wanted to have fun and remind everyone that life does go on. Emma knew that wouldn't be easy, but she was ready for a different life path than the one she'd been following. And she finally felt ready enough to take on whatever Gott was sending her.

She prayed in that moment. For forgiveness for herself and for Evan. For a new hope for Emily and peace for her parents. She prayed for a better life for all of the Troyer's and that their hearts would be healed. Above all, she prayed for Liam O'Shaughnessy. That he would wait for her until she was ready for him. Because she knew that she would wait for him... as long as it took.

AMISH TRUTH AND GRACE

MARISA MEYER

Nothing could have prepared Martha Yoder for the way things would change when her family decided they wanted to move to St Ignatius, an Amish settlement at the base of Mission Mountains. Miles away from her birth place and all she knew, she is thrown into a world where the rules were much different to the way she was raised as a child. The Old Order was precise, crimes were reprimanded and forgiveness was given for those who sought it. They had no reason to interact with Englischers or bother with their lost souls. But when she meets Jonah, the young man who returns their stolen horse, she starts to see a different side of grace. Suddenly she finds herself willing to help the destitute and she offers her services to take care of children at the shelter.

All he wanted to do, was make sure that Charlie returns the horse to the newcomers at St Ignatius, what Jonah didn't expect was to meet the stubborn and fiery Martha Yoder. He was well aware of the fact that the Old Order faith was deeply embedded in her heart and mind, and goes on a mission to show her that to have truth, you have to apply grace. What he didn't expect was to fall in love...

Chapter 1

The fog swirled low on the ground where the Mission Mountains rose from the valley floor and Martha's heart ached. It's been a week since their arrival at St Ignatius and still she struggled with the sudden change. Having had to leave all her friends behind, including Joseph, her life was irrevocably turned upside down. Out of the blue her parents her parents had decided it was time for change and she still had no inclination why. They were happy back in Ohio, or so she thought. Now she was thrown into this New Order where they worshiped in church buildings and where children road bicycles, and to make matters worse—there were at least three families who made use of electricity and she knows of one family who had a motor car. How could her parents even consider this to be right?

"Martha!" her mother called from inside the house.

She pretended not to hear and instead got up and walked toward the stables. Call it insolence, but right now she had no words. She wanted to go back home and if she took days or even weeks, she would make her parents see the error of their ways.

"Martha!"

"God help them see," she prayed silently as her mother called for her again before turning around and heading back to the house.

"You called?" she asked entering the kitchen.

"Where have you been?"

"I was outside."

"Come set the table, dinner is ready."

Martha shuffled over to the kitchen cupboard and took out three plates and the cutlery.

"Take out two more plates, Aunt Bethany and your uncle Stefan will be joining us."

Martha took a deep breath and guarded her tongue. Ever since they arrived here all her mother could talk about was her sister. She was certain it was her mother's idea to move here, and it was all because of

Aunt Bethany. She had been a member of St Ignatius since she could remember and whenever she came to visit them out at Ohio, she would boast about the freedom the Montana Amish offered. It was the work of the devil and she despised it. But she was in no position to voice her opinion. She would however pray for God's will to prevail. Sooner than later they will see how wrong they have been.

Dinner was interesting to say the least and although Martha had nothing to say, her mother seemed happy. Uncle Stefan spent the evening telling her father about the new tractor he bought to work the land. By the end of the evening, Martha had enough and excused herself. Instead of going to her room, she took her coat and in the dark made her way to the barn where the horses were kept.

Martha woke with a start and found herself asleep on a bale of hay in the barn with her bible spread open on her lap. She must have fallen asleep while she sought the solitude of the barn to get away from everything. Against the wood-paneled wall the oil lamp was flickering zealously and cast an arch of gold that enveloped her and chased away the blackness of the night. Picking up her bible she shoved it into her apron pocket and hooked the lantern off the wall. Her parents had been so bedazzled by the marvels of the western order and their new found freedom they hadn't even bothered to see if she was in her bed. Disappointed, she clicked her tongue and stalked towards the exit, but just then something caught her eye. One stall was standing wide open. She moved closer, raising the lantern to eye level. The closer she got the more restless the horses became. Ebony was especially anxious.

"What's the matter girl?" she whispered to try to settle the horse, but Ebony moved from side to side, nodding her head and hoofing the ground.

It was Autumn's stall door that stood wide open. Martha swallowed and sucked in a nervous breath and just as she moved to look into the stall, a man shouted and the horse bolted forward, knocking the lantern out of her hand and sending it flying across the barn floor. She screamed. It was simply terrifying.

"Daed! Daed! The horses!" she shouted towards the house. And it was when she spun around that she noticed the bright yellow glow coming from within the barn. Without a second thought she ran back inside. Smoke bellowing up into the air, choking her.

"Fire!" she cried. "Ebony!"

It was bad enough they had lost one of their horses to a thief but losing another would be a catastrophe.

Her father was first on the scene, panic stricken and shocked. A few neighbors had also joined to help while her mother took her aside as they watched on while everyone helped to get the blaze under control.

Chapter 2

The next day, Martha assessed the damage. It had been nothing short of a miracle, but still, this was God's way of punishing them, Martha thought. Although the damage was minimal, it was still unsightly. The entrance of the barn where the flames had licked hungrily was charred and soot spread out above the entrance like evil shadows reaching for the roof trusses. If it wasn't for that thief, none of this would have happened. She could still not fathom as to why her parents would still insist on staying. Was the writing on the wall not clear enough for them?

"It was quite a night," a man said, startling her.

She spun around, but the sun had settled right behind the man's head and all she could see was a faceless silhouette of the stranger.

"Excuse me?"

He tilted his head nodding slightly and then walked and came to stand beside her, leaning on the fence.

"Your horse is back in the barn by the way."

Surprised she looked at him. A smile tugged at the corners of his mouth and two distinct dimples sunk in on his cheeks. He was handsome, with longish blonde hair and blue but serious eyes. No, she would not be distracted by boyish charm.

"I know, I put her there myself."

He chuckled and then put two fingers in his mouth and whistled before saying, "I'm talking about the other one."

As she looked towards the barn again, a young man with hunched shoulders came walking towards them with Autumn in tow. Puzzled she glanced at the man beside her.

"You caught the thief?"

He ignored her question, but as the youngster came closer, he walked over to him and then stroked Autumn's mane as if it was his horse.

"Charlie, don't you have something to say to Miss Gruber?"

The young man shuffled uncomfortable, his eyes cast down and a frown worrying his brow. Martha watched curiously as the two exchanged glances and then the young man, named Charlie cleared his throat.

"I'm really sorry for the trouble I caused you ma'am."

Taken aback she frowned, "The trouble you caused," she looked from one man to the other, "I don't understand."

The other man stepped forward and extended his hand to her, "The name's Jonah, this here is Charlie, he was responsible for the incident last night."

"He's the horse thief!?"

"Oh no, no, I was just wanting to... well you see I wanted to ride her..." Charlie started but Jonah placed his hand on his shoulder.

"Charlie borrowed the horse, he wasn't expecting anyone to be there so when you woke up he panicked and..."

"Wait, you mean to say you people make a habit of borrowing other people's property without asking? Have you no dignity?"

Jonah patted Charlie on the shoulder and sent him on his way before he turned to Martha. From the first moment she spoke he could hear the indignation in her tone, which he found both amusing and worrying. She was from a very rigid Old Order church where grace and truth was not mentioned in the same sentence. But here in St Ignatius things were different. As a community, devoted to helping those in need, a few of them dedicated their lives in helping youngster such as Charlie to find purpose and teach them that there is much more to life than petty thievery and drug abuse.

"He apologized did he not?" Jonah asked.

"I don't care, he stole our horse," she said bluntly, "He should ask repentance of the church and the community or face shunning."

She was truly Old Order, he thought amusedly and shook his head.

"Fortunately for him, he's a heathen. So it's not up to the church to forgive him."

"You mean he's an Englischer?" she whispered in shock.

"That he is, and I believe as long as he's apologized to you, it should be your duty to forgive and not judge."

"But he stole Autumn..."

"... Borrowed, and he returned her."

"Yes but if it wasn't for him, this whole thing," she gestured to the barn, "would not have happened."

Jonah crossed his arms and stood with his feet apart. "I stand corrected, but if you were in bed, where a young lady is supposed to have been, you wouldn't even have noticed Autumn was gone. You wouldn't have ventured into the path of danger, and the place would never have caught fire."

That did it; she spun around without a single word and stormed off. With an amused smile he watched her leave. She was a piece of work, no doubt, but then again, so was he not too long ago. That was until he realized that grace and truth could never be separated. Grace without truth was reckless, forgiveness used to eliminate consequence, and truth without grace was shameful. When he was caught with a mobile phone, and refused to ask forgiveness, his community shunned him. No grace was found in their actions. They had been so focused on the truth they believed in, the fact that technology is from the devil that there was no common ground or understanding to be found. And when his sister was viciously attacked and critically wounded in her own home, it was the mobile phone and one call to the emergency services that saved her life. But even that was inconceivable for the elders of his church. And when he finally arrived here at St Ignatius and found their ways far more reasonable, he realized that he'd been living under a rock all this time. Finally he had forgiven himself and accept God's grace.

Chapter 3

"We are going back and that's final."

Martha stood in the hallway, biting her lip as she listened to her parents argue. Her mother was in tears and her father was angry. All this time she thought it was a decision they both had made, but as it was, it seemed like it was her mother who convinced him to come here. But now witnessing her mother's distress, her heart ached.

"Abram, we were not happy there, at least here we have family, people who care about us."

"So you'll run after foolish dreams and hopes instead of following God?"

"No! I would never!" her mother protested.

"So why can't we go back to the way things were?"

A chair scraped across the floor and Martha ducked into the linen closet in the hallway.

"Because I haven't seen my sister for almost eight years, and I haven't seen her children, I missed her!"

"But I'm your family now Eva, and if you do not wish to go back, then I will go back on my own, and I know for certain that Martha would follow. Will you stay here on your own then?"

Her mother sobbed and then she heard a loud bang with dishes clattering. "The go Abram! Go!"

The next moment the door to the kitchen slammed and all she could hear was her mother's sobbing. Everything was going wrong in their lives and all because of this place. But she couldn't help but feel sorry for her mother. She quietly crept out of the linen closet and made her way to the kitchen.

"*Mamm*, are you all right?"

Her mother didn't look up, simply sat at the kitchen table with her face buried in her arms. This was all her fault, she thought. She'd been so adamant that their ill-fortune was because of their choice to leave the Old Order; she hadn't noticed that her family was falling apart.

"Autumn is back in the barn," she whispered as she sat down next to her mother.

"He is?"

"Yes, a man brought him back this morning."

Her mother smiled through her tears and touched her hand, "I'm so glad to hear that. Your *daed* was so worried."

"An Englischer borrowed her." She couldn't believe the words coming out of her mouth. It almost sounded as if she was defending a crime, but she would do anything to ease her mother's pain. "He said he only wanted to ride her."

Her mother wiped the tears from her cheeks with the tips of her fingers, "That's wonderful news."

Martha nodded, she fought the urge to tell her mother what was really on her mind, but instead she sat quietly comforting her mother in silence. Sometimes words can do more harm than good, and right now nothing she said or did would make her mother feel any better about their predicament. At least now she knew her father would for certain take them back to their home.

Much later that morning she found herself stuck in a room full of other women for their weekly quilting session. She had learned that they were making blankets for a rehabilitation center settled on an Englischer' s farm a few miles from St Ignatius. She had to admit; knowing she was contributing to such a noble cause felt good. As she watched the women work merrily whilst chatting away, a slight knot formed in her stomach. Even with all that was going on, being here wasn't all that bad, it wasn't home, but it was also not godless.

"So how are you finding your new home?"

It was Liza, one of the younger girls, about her age, who came to sit next to her.

"Oh it's all right," she shrugged, "It's different."

"I believe so. *Mamm* said they are much stricter."

Martha raised a brow, "It's for the sake of the eternal soul, without rules we would not find heaven."

Liza laughed, "And having an outhouse instead of indoor plumbing would keep you from heaven?"

Martha pursed her lips and turned her attention to her quilting, hoping that Liza would just go about her way, but she sat closer, almost intrigued.

"I hear Jonah brought your horse back."

So this was what she really wanted to talk about, Martha realized but refused to respond.

"He helps out at the rehabilitation center; he has such a kind soul." Liza sighed wistfully. "The woman he marries one day would be blessed. He's just so handsome too."

Liza's unbearable babble was getting on Martha's nerves but she would not allow such a trivial matter to upset her.

"Charlie brought the horse back," she said blankly and then set her quilt aside and stood up. "*Mamm*," she said turning to her mother, "I'm not feeling so well, I'm going home."

Chapter 4

Jonah was more than just intrigued by Martha. To him, her stubbornness was a sign of strength and determination, and he admired that. Not to mention she was a beautiful woman. Her hair always so neatly plated and tucked under her bonnet with the brightest blue eyes that can challenge any storm.

As he made his way to his house, he noticed her exiting Liza's home where the women in the community normally gathered to work on quilts. It was rather unexpected since he didn't expect her to want to get involved. From the brief exchange he had with her, she wasn't happy at being here.

"Martha!" he called as he jogged over to her.

She paused, didn't look around but her head tilted slightly and she picked up her pace walking away from him. But he would not give up this easily. When he finally caught up to her, he fell into step beside her.

"I see you've met Liza?"

"I have."

"Are you joining them with quilting?"

"No."

He smiled. She was obviously trying to get rid of him, but he wouldn't give up so easily. As they passed the line of buggies that stretched before them on the road he kept up with her, despite her cold shouldered manner. It was time he showed her where truth and grace met; she was far too beautiful to remain so ignorant.

They had almost passed his buggy when he placed his hand gently under her elbow, her startled gaze shot to him and he shrugged.

"I want to show you something."

Her eyes as wide as saucers she looked up at him, "You have nothing to show me, let me go."

He smirked and without warning, cupped his hands around her waist and effortlessly hoisted her on to the passenger seat of the buggy. He half expected her to kick him, or at least shove him away from her, but by the look of utter shock and disbelief he was convinced that he had shocked her into a petrified state.

"You'll like it, I promise," or hope, "It won't take long."

He could feel her eyes follow him as he moved around in front of the horses to get to the driver's side and eyed her for a second. He would give her one more chance to make a run for it, and when all she did was stare at him he chuckled and set the buggy in motion.

A short while later, just over the hill, the shelter came into focus, the white wooden barn shaped house where the destitute and desperate from all over comes to find purpose. It stood alone in the valley, surrounded by the most picturesque beauty, green lawns and flowerbeds surrounded the place. A plant nursery lay to the left of the house and angled up the hill and to the right was a vegetable patch maintained by the regulars that lived here.

"It's beautiful..." she whispered, barely audible.

Surprised by her reaction, he smiled. "That it is, come I want to show you around," he said once he parked his buggy in the designated area and helped her down. "Welcome to Serenity."

He could tell that she was hesitant, but also noticed the flicker of intrigue in her eyes. If she could see how wonderful this place is, and what they do to help the homeless and destitute she would change her opinion of St Ignatius and hopefully of him.

They made their way up the wooden stairs and into the building.

"This place was established about four years ago," he said and nodded at two men passing by.

"But why?" she asked curiously, her eyes darting from one thing to the other.

"Well, as a community we realized the need to shine God's light to the world, and the only way to do that is what He expects of us. Whoever closes his ear to the cry of the poor will himself call out and not be answered," he quoted from the bible. "You see, it is our duty as followers of God to show those who do not know better what it means to serve a loving God…"

He hadn't noticed that he'd walked ahead of her and only when he turned around did he notice her standing at one of the doors that lead off the main hallway. It was the daycare room where all the children gathered during the day while their parents went out to seek employment. The colorful walls filled with drawings and children paintings brightened the place up and made it look lively. Kids from as little as two years, all played together. Some building structures with handmade wooden building blocks, others painting and drawing and some of the older ones reading.

"This is the daycare. A lot of these children have never had a home of their own or a bed to sleep in. This," he gestured, "Is the one place where they are protected from the elements and cruelty of the world."

She tilted her head, and he met her glistening eyes. Something in her expression had turned from apathy to empathy and seeing that fraction of grace depicted in the windows of her soul touched him.

"There are so many of them," she whispered.

"This is actually not that many, when winter draws near there is a lot more. By the end of the year we will build another dormitory to accommodate everyone and we will have no reason to show anyone away."

"You have to show children away?" she gasped.

He laughed, "No, we never do, but the older people we try to place elsewhere if we can. Some of the families in our community often offer to help with accommodation when Serenity has no space."

He watched her and he could tell her mind was working overtime. He didn't expect her to understand what they do and why, but he knew the shields that covered her eyes were slowly starting to peel away.

Chapter 5

A few weeks had gone by and already she had visited Serenity twice, mostly to spend time in the daycare center with the children. She was always fond of children and now being part of something greater, she was realizing just how one-track minded she was. All this time locked away behind rules and regulations. Seeing Englischer as heathen and keeping evil outside of their protected community. It had been after her very first visit to this place she had prayed and asking God for guidance and her decision to volunteer felt right.

"Where are you going?" her dad demanded when she headed out the door.

She spun around, she was so raptured in her own thoughts she hadn't noticed him sitting in the living room. "I'm going to the shelter."

Her dad stood up and tucked his thumbs under his suspenders. The frown that drew his brows together carved into his forehead. "I don't want you to go there."

"But *Daed*, I'm helping the *Kinner*."

He raised a brow and cleared his throat, "I forbid you to go."

"But I made a promise!"

"Do not disrespect me, I have spoken."

Martha's heart sank, she was looking forward to her day at Serenity. For the first time in her life she felt rebellious, she really shouldn't feel this way and reject her parent's wishes, but not going, felt like she was breaking a promise, not only to the children, but to God.

She raised her chin and looked at him and said, "Do not hinder the children, for the Kingdom of God belongs to them."

Her father gritted his teeth, "You will be so determined to undermine me, your father, the head of the household?"

"Abram, let her go and see to the *kinner*, she's doing a good thing and God expects that of her."

It was her mom who entered the living room an stood between the two of them.

"So now you are also defying me," he muttered.

"No," her mother said, "I am not, I am honoring God and you are hindering his work." To Martha she nodded, "Jonah is outside, go."

She didn't wait, with a quick glance to her mother and then her father, she hurried outside.

"Good morning Martha," Jonah said with a big smile, "I trust you are having a good morning so far?"

He was always so positive, she thought. It didn't seem like anything on this planet could break his spirit.

"I will call it a good morning the day my *daed* accepts the fact that I'm a grown woman."

Jonah burst out laughing. "To him you will always be his little girl Martha."

Her heart pounded in her chest and a swirl of butterflies swarmed around in her stomach. It happened every time he said her name; it ran off his tongue like warm honey. She fought for control and crossed her hands on her lap.

"Well I'm not a little girl, I'm a grown woman," she muttered.

"I don't doubt that for one moment."

She made the mistake of looking at him and her heart rate exploded, so much so, it felt as if every beat of her heart was squeezing the air from her lungs. It had nothing to do with the fact that he was handsome, or charming to an extent, but it had everything to do with the fact that she was falling in love. As that realization swept over her like torrential rains she whipped her head around and looked at the road instead.

She couldn't possibly have these feelings for him, could she? But all the way to Serenity she couldn't deny that she enjoyed his company and his closeness. Matters had simply gotten out of control.

When they finally reached Serenity, she didn't wait for him to help our out of the buggy, she swung her legs over the side and leaped to the ground, not bothering with the step to gracefully lower herself down.

If only she had waited. The moment she landed on the ground, she stepped on a stone, her ankle twisted and she toppled over. How Jonah managed to get from the other side of the buggy to her so quickly was beyond her.

"Martha, are you all right?" Concern etched on his face as he reached to help her up.

"Yah, I'm all right, I lost my footing," she fibbed but as she stood on her right foot a sharp pain shot from her ankle all the way up to her knee. "Ouch!" she cried out and immediately took the pressure off her foot, but Jonah had his arm around her waist helped her back on to the buggy seat.

"Here let me take a look."

The moment he reached for her foot she flinched, not out of pain but how gently he had lifted her foot. Her heel rested in the palm of his hand.

"I have to take your shoe and sock off," he said and looked up at her for approval.

She really shouldn't let him; it all fell far too intimate. "I'm sure it's nothing," she whispered trying to keep her dress in place.

She saw understanding flash in his eyes and he straightened up and carefully let go of her foot. "I will carry you to the nurse's station and have the doctor take a look then."

Martha nodded, but this seemed more intimate than him looking at her bare foot. And as he slid one arm around her back and wedged the other under her knees, drawing her into his arms, her world swirled into oblivion. If her father were to see this, he would drag her before the council and have her punished for her unchaste ways. Regardless of her injured foot, he would never tolerate this behavior.

"It's a bad sprain Martha," the Englisch doctor said as he examined her foot. "There isn't much one can do in this case, other than RICE."

"Rice?" she asked puzzled, how would rice help a sprained foot.

She looked over to where Jonah stood, his mouth hidden behind his hand, but she could see a smile tugging at the corners of his mouth by the way his cheeks pulled up.

"Rest, Ice, Compression and Elevation," the doctor said and smiled. "I have a set of crutches you can use for when you need to move around, but I suggest we rest your foot for most of today."

"You mean to say I have to sit all day?" she asked irritably.

"I'm afraid so. Jonah told me you help out at the daycare center?"

She watched him as he wrapped a bandage around her ankle and she shifted to sit up slightly.

"Yes," she simply said biting her lip. Although the doctor was being careful, the pain was near unbearable. "Are you sure it isn't broken?"

He smiled and then carefully put her sock over the bandaged foot. "It's not broken although it could be just as painful, once the swelling is down it will already feel a lot better."

"I will take you back to your home," Jonah suggested as he stepped closer, "You would need to rest your foot."

"But I can still help, I'm not ill."

"The *kinner* will be too busy, and I don't want you hurt any more than you already are."

He had a point, they could get rather excited when they played and she often found herself huddled on the floor amongst them. Disappointed, she allowed Jonah to take her back home.

Chapter 6

What began as a light drizzle of rain two days ago soon turned into a storm. The wind howled through the tree tops, bending their thick trunks like twigs, causing the lower hanging branches to reach dangerously to the ground, while torrential rains flooded the landscape. Serenity had been flooded with people seeking shelter and after the high intake of destitute homeless people, he was exhausted. Over and above that the director of Serenity had spoken to him about Martha and the fact that she wasn't a qualified councilor. He had opposed it, but there wasn't much he could do. Most of the people who worked at the shelter had some sort of in-house training, especially the Amish volunteers, like cooks and caretakers, but for teaching and counselling it had been mostly Englischer with degrees and diplomas.

The rain had damaged parts of the dirt road, making it near impossible to drive on, but he needed to get home. He had offered to take Martha to the frolicking so she could get out a bit, but at this rate he doubted he would get there in time. And up ahead the road looked as if God had erased the landscape. With nothing but a lantern guiding his way; it was difficult to see, but he travelled this road daily and he knew he could find his way even if he was blind. He navigated his buggy carefully through the storm hoping he wouldn't run into any trouble. It was difficult to hear above the downpour of rain, but just a mile or so outside St Ignatius he heard the fain cry of someone in trouble. He stopped and listened. There it was again.

"Help!"

"Hello, where are you?!" he called into the storm.

"Help!"

It was a man, but with minimal visibility he couldn't see a thing.

"Keep shouting, so I can get to you!" he called.

The man cried out again and again and Jonah used that as a guide to reach him. As he drew closer to where the cries for help came from he saw the black outline of a buggy lying on its side with the horses trotting nervously on the spot. Jonah rushed over, sliding down the embankment as careful as he could. When he finally got to the injured man, he noticed with shock it was Martha's father.

"Mr Yoder, it's me Jonah, can you tell me where it hurts?" he asked as he tried to assess the situation.

"My leg..." he groaned, "It's caught under the buggy."

Jonah raised the lantern to where his leg was caught. With such little light it was hard to see if it was crushed or broken or just stuck, but he had to free him. He looked around for anything to use as leverage and spotted a branch not too far away.

"Hold on, I'll get you freed in no time, he said and place the lantern next to Mr Yoder."

With some effort, he finally managed to lever the buggy enough for Mr Yoder to drag his leg out from under the heavy load and got him to the safety of his own buggy.

"What were you doing on the road in this storm?" he asked as they got on their way.

Martha's dad didn't answer him, simply sat, clutching his leg and groaning in agonizing pain. But the fact that he was here, had Jonah thinking. Would he have gone to speak to the director to prevent Martha from working at the shelter? He hated to think that her father would go to such lengths, but it was possible. He'd met him twice since their arrival and he knew Mr Yoder wasn't keen on being here in St Ignatius or on the fact that his daughter was mingling with Englischers on a social level.

When they reached the Yoder home, and Jonah helped Mr Yoder to the front door, it was Eva who instantly jumped in to help.

"Abram you foolish man, what have you gone and done?"

"It's no-one's business but my own Eva, just get me to a chair."

"Mr Yoder, I will call for the doctor to come see to your leg," Jonah offered.

"No, my leg is fine, I will rest it."

Jonah knew better, the injury on his leg was far worse than he would like to admit, but he wouldn't go against and elder's wishes.

Eva waked him to the front door and when they were out of range she whispered, "I'll get Martha, she was looking forward to joining you at the sing. You will take good care of her yah?"

He smiled down at the fragile looking woman, who was an older version of her daughter.

"I will, my intentions are honorable Mrs. Yoder."

"Good, good. Now go wait outside."

Before long, Martha came around the back of the house. She was dressed in a plain lilac dress and a smile spread across her lips. With a raincoat covering her head and shoulders she ran towards the buggy and instinctively Jonah hoisted her into it and out of the rain.

"Is your foot better then?" he asked as he got in next to her.

"Evening to you too Jonah," she said playfully. "My foot is much better, the swelling has gone down."

He laughed, "And now your father has taken a turn at injuring himself, I'd almost say this is planned."

She laughed and shook her head, "I do not know why on earth he would have been out in this rain, where did you find him."

Jonah knew he should tell her about his suspicions but he couldn't possible cause a rift between father and daughter.

"On my way here, I think his buggy veered off the road and got caught in a ditch."

"He can be very foolish at times."

Jonah smiled and didn't speak another word about the incident as they made their way to the church.

Chapter 7

Jonah's visit had become a regular occurrence and the more Martha got to know him the fonder she had become. But she missed her regular visits to Serenity. In the short time she got to spend with the children at the daycare had given her a new outlook on life. During one of her visits there she also got to meet the horse thief, Charlie. At first it had been hard for her to look at him with no judgement, but then she learned that he was a troubled teenager, thrown away by his birth parents and left to fend for himself. And with the help of Serenity and Jonah, he was slowly starting to grow into a young responsible man.

It was on Wednesday morning when she had enough of sitting at home and going to Quilting meetings. Outside the birds were chirping, signaling the dawn of a new day. Her father, still bed ridden after the wound on his leg got septic and he was forced to seek medical help, had seemingly turned over a new leaf. There was no more talk of returning to their old home, instead, he was planning on starting up his own furniture making business, like he always wanted. Her mother of course believed it was God's intervention and all her prayers that changed his heart.

"*Mamm*, I want to go to the *kinner* at Serenity today," she said over breakfast.

Her mother paused and quietly set down her spoon. "I don't think it's wise for you to get involved with those *kinner*, they will grow attached to you."

"And so?" she asked curiously, "They have no one else."

"I know Martha, but you're not qualified."

Martha huffed and sat back in her chair, "Since when does one need to be qualified to see to *kinner*?"

A sound behind her made her look around and her father stood in the doorway, leaning heavily against the door jamb.

"Martha, I spoke to the director at Serenity. It is no place for a young unwed woman to be. There are too many immoral young men there, and they may be there for help, but they are Englischers and their intentions are not honorable."

She couldn't believe her ears. Her father kept on talking but it sounded like a rushing river swooshing around in her head drowning out his voice.

She interrupted him mid-sentence, "So that's where you were when Jonah found you?"

Her mother lowered her head, and her father couldn't look her in the eyes.

"You went behind my back and ruined my future in helping those *kinner* who needs God more than you and I?"

"Martha, please, I was merely looking out for you. If you were wed, then it would be different, but you're young, and those men there, I have seen the way they look at the other women at Serenity."

"Stop! Just stop! *Daed*, I'm not a child anymore, I'm twenty-two, and I can protect myself..."

She was so angry and so busy stating the facts she didn't hear the knock on the door, or care when her mother got up to go see who it is.

"... so my unwed status is keeping me from serving God? Is that how it is now? Well then..." she started and stood up, raising her chin defiantly, "If that's the case I will just have to marry Jonah," she blurted out.

The sound of a man clearing his throat behind her startled her, and she cringed inwardly as she turned to follow her father's surprised gaze, only to see Jonah standing there with his arms crossed over his chest and his legs apart, with a smile tugging at his mouth. Her mother averted her gaze and cupped her hand over her mouth, obviously fighting off a giggle and she could feel the rush of heat make its way up to her cheeks.

"Good morning Martha," he said smiling and then greeted her father, "Mr Yoder, I see you are up and about?"

Martha was mortified, and instead of greeting him she darted past him and ran outside. How could she have been so childish to blabber such things out in the heat of the moment. Ever since her arrival here in St Ignatius she had transformed from the obedient daughter, to a rebellious riffraff who keeps getting herself into trouble. She had lost her way, and the further she veered off the path of faith the harder it would be to return. Rumspringa, she thought. A word she wouldn't have dared to utter before. Maybe she would go and experience life in the modern world instead. Get away from this place and discover life outside the fold. But even as those thoughts flooded her, her soul protested. No, she couldn't. She could never leave her family behind, and besides, she had no friends who would be willing to do this with her. Confused she sunk down on a bale of hay and cupped her hands over her face.

"Martha?"

Great! Jonah had to follow her here.

"Go away, I don't want to talk to you," she mumbled.

"I don't think you really want me to leave."

She whipped her head up and glared at him, "What makes you think I want you to stay?"

He walked closer and went down on his haunches before her, his arms resting on his knees as he looked at her.

"For one, you enjoy my company, you said so yourself. And I want to marry you."

Martha's head spun. Did he just say he wanted to marry her?

"What on earth are you talking about, you don't want to marry me, you just feel sorry for me. You heard what I said, and just because I would marry to be able to work at Serenity, doesn't mean it would be a happy marriage. You don't even love me!"

He smiled and gently took her hand in his before standing up and pulling her to her feet.

"That's where you are wrong. I knew about your father's visit to the Director at Serenity, and I also knew the only way I could have you close to me is if you worked there. So..." he started as he led her out of the barn. "This morning when I woke up, I knew exactly what I wanted. I want you to be my wife, to work with me at Serenity and serve God the way a husband and wife should serve him."

Martha's heart skipped a beat, and she brought her hand to her chest. How was this even possible? A few weeks ago, she couldn't stand him, and then she got to know him and he taught her how one could not have truth and grace could not function without the other. He taught her to look past the label of heathen and Englischers and showed her how each person is part of God's creation. More than anything he showed her a love that exceeds normal understanding.

"Are you sure this is what you want?" she asked hesitantly.

Jonah chuckled and cupped her face, "From the first day I met you, I knew we were meant to be together."

Martha's eyes shot full of tears and through the tears she smiled and wrapped her arms around Jonah's waist. Fearing that her words may fail her, she simply held on to him.